Ménage à Quatre

and tales of sexy threesomes

by

Misty MacAllister

TABLE OF CONTENTS

Ménage à Quatre

"How's it going, Mrs. Carlisle?" Rick asked, looking me up and down with his beautiful, big brown eyes.

He was pushing the mower and grinning. He seemed happy with what he was seeing.

It was early—before seven—on a Monday. The last time I saw virgin morning on Monday I had been awake all night Sunday, but this morning I had a very good reason to drag myself out of bed. Lust!

"Oh, please, Rick. You've known me long enough to call me Anna," I said, walking over to one of the loungers by the pool.

"Sure, Anna," he said. "I'm going to do some yard work. Is that ok with you?"

He gave me a hungry young man glance that was so straightforward, it sent shivers through me. I was in a white one-piece that pushed up my tits and crawled up my ass. His lustful look said I was still something to look at. Even at thirty-three. Keep looking, big boy!

"Do what you have to do, don't worry about me, Rick," I said, turning to bend over the lounger and giving him a good look at my juicy ass. "I'm going to sit here and do a bit of reading."

Rick grew up right down the street, and my hubby, Victor, the skinflint, had hired him because, as he had said, it gave the boy something to do. In reality, it was because Rick was cheaper than a lawn service and he worked like a dog. He had been doing the lawn regularly for four years, and he had barely turned eighteen. He certainly wasn't a boy anymore.

7

He was a buff man, and he was why I was awake so early.

"Ok, Mrs....Anna," he said, smiling. "Feel free to tell me if I'm bothering you."

Uh, huh, hot and bothering.

"I will," I said, unable to take my eyes off him.

His brown hair was wavy and a little shaggy. His face was angular. He had a dimple on his left cheek. Rick was definitely a heartthrob—actually, it wasn't my heart that he made throb, but cuntthrob just doesn't have the same ring.

He pulled off his t-shirt. Drooling, I watched his muscles work. Oh my, rippling stomach and chiseled pecs—good morning, beautiful world! I was getting wet just from looking at him. He dropped the t-shirt on the ground.

"Is that what you do with your clothes, Rick?" I said. "Give me that."

He grinned. "You're like my mom, Anna," he said, tossing me his t-shirt—and I wanted to tell him that I was nothing like his mom, unless she wanted to suck her son's cock. "She hates how I leave my clothes everywhere."

I caught his t-shirt. "Aren't you cold?" I asked, looking up at his razor sharp little nipples. God, I wanted to bite them!

"No way. It feels great out here," he said, stretching.

"Brrr," I said, shivering from the temperature and my libido. Thank

8

God, it was cool, because it meant I could use the throw to cover myself.

"Don't let me keep you. I know you must have better things to do on your Easter break."

"Not really," he said. "I'm taking it easy."

"I bet you are," I said. "I bet the girls are lined up to be with you."

He smiled. "I don't have the time to date," he said. "I've got to think about school."

"Well, don't work too hard," I said, arranging my blanket so he couldn't see where my hand was going. "This is the time to have fun."

"That's what everyone says," he laughed, and he pushed the mower toward the lawn.

I watched him go. His cut-offs were booty shorts, and his firm ass looked so damn hot. I breathed in his scent from his t-shirt. It was musky.

I'm a dirty old lady lusting after a sweet young piece of meat, I thought. I'm not getting enough sex, I thought.

Neither thought kept me from massaging my eager pussy beneath the throw. Did I care that I was outside? Did I care that I could see the houses across the lake? Did I care that anyone could see me? Fuck no.

**

The morning went on. The day got warmer. I watched Rick get sweaty, and I got hotter. He was so sexy, it was almost criminal. While he worked, I rubbed my mound. He mowed the lawn, and then he trimmed the bushes. I had a bush I'd have loved for him to trim. Not that my neat little thatch needed trimming, but my cunt could sure use some plowing. I was so horny!

By the time he was raking up the leaves, I had my knees bent and two fingers in my snatch. I was pumping away at my hot pussy, and I didn't care if he saw. At one point he was stretching while rubbing his hand across his six-pack. Watching, I frantically rubbed my clit as his fingers dipped down toward his joystick. I felt like a dirty perv, but the site was so sexy that I came right there in the backyard. While watching the yard boy and fingering myself. It was so wrong, but my orgasm was cataclysmic, like the Big Bang.

"That's it, Mrs. Carlisle," he called, coming over to me while I was still riding the rapturous rollercoaster.

I was flushed like a popped cherry when I looked up at his perfect body and beautiful face, and I had a finger still in my throbbing pussy, but what could the poor lady do?

"You did a great job, Rick," I breathed. I was panting, and he was the one who had been working. "Let me get you something." Or you can get me something. Some dick, I thought to myself.

"Mr. Carlisle already paid me," he said.

I shook my head. *He didn't pay you for what you did for me,* I wanted to say.

"No, he doesn't pay you enough for all you do," I said, getting up.

Rick looked sheepish. He knew Victor was a cheapskate, but he didn't want to say it.

"I insist," I said. "Let me grab my purse. It's inside. Come on."

I got up and sashayed toward the house.

He followed behind me, and all I could think was how my thighs were slick with cum and how he was watching my ass. Did he see a big wet spot on my ass? God, I hoped not. Then again, maybe it would give him ideas and he'd take the chance to fuck me right now.

There was something wrong with me. I was terminally horny, and the only cure was to be pounded by an eighteen-year-old dick.

I hesitated at the glass doors, looking at his reflection over my shoulder. His eyes were down. Assward. So he was looking, which was encouraging, but he didn't take me. I slid open the door and stepped back into him 'accidentally'. Right!

"Sorry," I said, reaching out to catch myself by grabbing his ass.

His big strong hands caught my hips as my butt bumped against his crotch. His body was hard. He smelled like sweat and grass. Did I feel something hard in his shorts? For what seemed like an eternity, I didn't move.

Fuck me! Fuck me! I was thinking, but he just held on. Maybe he did think of me as his mom.

"Come on," I finally breathed, and I went in the house.

Inside, it was even cooler than outside, and my nipples were suddenly rockets. They were so hard, they hurt. They needed squeezing, or biting. I pointed them at Rick. He stared.

"Are you coming to the BBQ for Easter?" I asked.

Victor was a big one for cooking with fire outside, and he liked an audience. For the Easter weekend he invited the whole street.

"I wouldn't miss it," Rick said, his eyes locked on my perky tits.

When I met Victor, he loved my tits. They're 34 C, round, with pouty, perky nipples. They're nice, but I always liked my ass.

I found my purse and gave Rick a twenty.

"Thanks, Anna," he said, taking the bill.

"Anytime," I said. But what I wanted to say was: I can give you so much more!

After he left, I scooted my ass up on the kitchen island and gave my lady the attention she deserved. I used the handle of a whisk instead of the dick I wanted. The granite was cold under my ass as I pounded my little pussy, fantasizing about hard-body Rick.

**

That night, when Victor got home, I met him at the door in lingerie, and I was blowing him before he even shut the door.

"That's fucking great, Anna," he grunted when I had his little chubby in my mouth.

Victor had a nice cock, nothing special, five inches, reasonably thick, and eager. I just didn't see it enough. I sucked his dick while he pulled off his clothes. He grabbed the back of my head and pounded my mouth. I swallowed him whole, but I wanted more. I pulled away.

"Fuck me, Vic," I moaned.

Vic was close to Rick, and they were both close to dick, which was what I desperately needed.

I pulled away and got in front of him on all fours. I wiggled my ass up at him.

"Right here?" he asks.

The front door was closed, but it was glass. Unfortunately, the house was off the street, and the glass was treated to be one way. No one could see us. And I wished so badly that someone could see us. What I wanted right now was to be bad. I'd love it if Victor fucked me in the street so the whole neighborhood could see.

"Fuck me, Vic," I insisted, wiggling my butt and fingering my pussy. He fell to his knees and gave me what I wanted, sliding his dick in my wet canal. He thrust to the hilt. It felt good.

"Harder," I demanded.

He pulled out and thrust back. He was holding my hips, but his hands weren't grabbing me the way I wanted. I wanted him to fucking take me!

"Harder," I grunted. "Fuck me, Rick."

Whoops. Did I say, Rick?

Vic didn't notice. He was thrusting now. Finding a rhythm. I wanted more. Needed more. I want him to spank my ass. I wanted him to treat me like a whore. I wanted him to use me. I grabbed my ass and started fingering that other tight hole.

It had been ten years since Vic took that back door. All I had for it was one of my silicone boyfriends.

"Fuck, Anna," he grunted.

My fingering my own hole was too much stimulation for Vic. He shuddered, thrust, and came.

Eight thrusts—I counted—and he was done.

I needed more.

**

The BBQ was a success. Practically the whole neighborhood was playing in the pool, or on the lake.

Rick was there. He was wearing a tight little cock-hugging bathing suit that showed me exactly what I was missing. Oh, boy. It was all I could do not to rip off the trunks and gobble his cock up like a fairy-tale witch.

It was torture hanging on Vic's arm while he schmoozed. I couldn't take my eyes off Rick. He was playing around with a girl from down the street. She was seventeen and had a seventeen-year-old's tight little body. I could tell by the outline in Rick's shorts that he liked her. Bulge. I was jealous of this little girl.

I watched Rick and the little slut splash around the pool. I watched the shameless whore push her perky teen titties against his arm. I watched her lean in close and whisper something that made him smile. Probably their plans to fuck later. And all I could do was stand behind Vic and rub my pussy hoping nobody would notice.

Finally, it was more than I could take. I told Vic I had a headache and had to go inside and lie down for a while.

"Sure, hon," he said. He didn't care. He was the life of the party. He had what he wanted.

What I wanted was a big dick.

I went inside. The house was quiet and cool. The party was all outside. I walked through the house. The walls were almost all glass, and I could see the party outside, but they couldn't see me. I went to the master bedroom. As I crossed the room, I pulled off the bandeau cover-up dress and threw it on the bed. In my tiny bikini, I went to the wall of windows. Standing there, I pushed the thong over and freed my mound.

I needed some relief.

I gingerly fingered my already wet, deprived pussy, and looked for Rick's hard body. I saw Vic. He was less than ten feet away at his huge smoker. He had his oversized boy toy, why couldn't I have mine?

I fingered my lady and looked for Rick. He was nowhere to be seen. No doubt he was off fucking that little tramp somewhere, damn her. She was probably a virgin, and he was popping her sweet cherry. How could I compete?

I leaned against the glass and rubbed my wet slit when I heard my name.

"Anna."

I jumped and pulled my hand away from my pussy, as if I had been caught fucking by my parents. I spun around. Rick was standing at the bedroom door, looking at me and smiling.

"Rick, what are you doing here?" I gasped.

"I saw you come inside," he said.

"I was just…" I started, but what was I going to say? That I had come inside to masturbate because I needed some dick? Your dick?

"I know what you're doing," he said, and he was stroking the bulge in those tight shorts.

The massive bulge!

Gulp.

"You do?" I gasped, unable to take my eyes off his trunks.

I was shaking, and my pussy was throbbing. Rick was here, and I could see what he wanted. Me!

"I know what you need," he said, and he walked into the room, pushing down his trunks.

His huge cock sprung up. It was easily twice the size of Vic's dick. Looking at it, I wanted to break out into the happy dick song.

He was going to give me what I needed. Yes!

Then another boy came into the room. He was an inch or two shorter than Rick's six two. He was black, clean cut, and already naked. His huge dick—not as big as Rick's, but it had to be nine inches—was throbbing as he stroked it. He was looking at me with hungry dark eyes. Another boy followed him. This one was blond and Hollywood good-looking. He was the shortest, less than six feet, and his exposed cock was a respectable seven inches. The three boys looked at me.

Oh boy!

My heart was thrumming.

"What's going on, Rick?" I said, making an effort to look at his eyes and not at his ginormous dick.

He shrugged his powerful shoulders. "We thought you might want to have fun, Anna," he said.

"What kind of fun do you have in mind?" I asked.

It was stupid question. Three hard dicks proclaimed quite clearly what they wanted to do, and they wanted to do it to me.

"The same kind you want, Anna," he said.

17

"I think I should go back to the party," I said, walking past Rick. The other boys moved out of the way.

"I just thought from the way you were fingering yourself earlier and the way you came watching me the other day that you wanted something more," Rick said.

I stopped. They were all so close.

"How old are you, boys?" I asked.

"We're all eighteen, Anna," Rick said.

"You know my husband's right outside," I said.

"I know," Rick said.

I licked my lips. My mouth was dry. My heart was beating a thousand miles a minute. I was suddenly scared, but these boys weren't going to rape me. They weren't going to do anything, unless I let them, but it was how much I wanted to let them do things to me that was scaring me.

"Do you really want to go, Anna?" Rick asked, sliding so close behind me that his cock brushed my ass.

I let out a whimper.

This was when I should have used my thinking brain and said, You bet I do, but I wasn't thinking, at least not with my head. All I could see were the strong, young, beautiful bodies so close to me. I looked down at the black guy's cock, and the head was swelling as he stroked the shaft. I was so hot. I couldn't take it anymore. It felt as if I was going

18

crazy.

"No," I whispered.

"What do you want?" Rick asked.

"I want you to give me what I need," I whispered.
Rick took me by the waist and pressed against my back, his massive cock sliding between my legs and rubbing over my wet slit.

"You want to be our whore, Anna?" he whispered in my ear.

His breath sent shivers down my spine. I squeezed my legs around his cock. I leaned back into him and closed my eyes. His body felt so right pressed against mine.

"Make me your whore," I hissed.

And that was enough for them. Their hands were suddenly all over me, grabbing my breasts, pinching my nipples, cupping my mound. Rick held my hips, and I rode his cock, letting it slip over my mound. He grunted. My bikini top was ripped off, and the thong practically disintegrated in their strong hands. I stood there, letting them touch me, and I thought that this was how it was going to be. They were so young, they couldn't wait. They would ravish me, and it would be over.

But I didn't want a fast fucking. I got that with Vic.

Then the hands were gone. Even Rick pulled away. With the hands gone, I suddenly felt naked.

"Open your eyes, Anna," Rick ordered. His playful voice was gone. This was the voice of a man.

I opened my eyes. They were standing about an arm's length away, watching me. I turned to face Rick. His rock-hard cock was slick with my juice.

"Get on your knees, Anna," he ordered.

"My knees?" I whispered.

Rick leaned forward and slapped me. It happened so fast I couldn't even move. It wasn't hard. It didn't even hurt. But it got my attention and made my heart beat so hard, it nearly hurt.

"Get on your knees, whore," he ordered.

Whore. That was me.

I dropped to my knees and crawled to him.

"Suck it," he ordered, waving his huge cock at me.

I reached out, and he slapped me again.

"No hands, whore," he snapped.

"Yes, master," I moaned, not even thinking what I was saying, and I leaned forward and caught his cock in my lips. It was so thick, it was hard to get my mouth around it.

"Look at me, whore," he said.

I looked up into his eyes.

"Do you like it?" he asked.
"Yes, I do," I said, stopping the sucking, and he slapped me again.

"Did I tell you to stop?" he said.

I shook my head and took him back in my mouth.

"Don't forget us, slut," the blond guy barked.

He and the black guy were on either side of me, their dicks poking at my face. I reached up to grab their cocks, but Rick slapped my hand. "No hands, whore," he said.

He grabbed my head and started fucking my face, thrusting his cock deep in my mouth till I gagged.

"You can suck cock, Anna," he moaned, pulling out his cock and thrusting it back in.

"Why don't you share the whore?" the blond complained.

"You want some?" Rick asked.

"Fuck, yeah," the blond said.

Rick pulled out of my mouth and turned my head to the blond, and his seven-inch cock slid into my mouth and down my throat. Rick held my head and pushed me down till my nose was pressed into the blond thatch of pubic hair.

"Fuck," the blond moaned.

I gagged, and Rick let go of my head. I pulled back and gulped air. Then the blond guy started fucking my mouth, and Rick rubbed the head of his cock on my cheek. I was being treated like a whore, and it was driving me wild. I sucked and fingered my swollen clit.

"Swallow me, whore," the blond guy grunted as I deep-throated his cock.

"Fuck you, guys," the black guy growled. "It's always like this."

Rick and the blond guy laughed. The black guy grabbed me by the middle and pulled me up off the blond guy's cock. It came out of my mouth with a loud slurp, and I was being flipped in the air like I was a doll. Before I knew it, I was upside down with my pussy up and my head down.

The black guy's big dick was in my face, so I did what a whore does. I started sucking. The black guy buried his face in my cunt, licking like a doggie. I grabbed his firm ass and did my best to take in the length of his huge cock.

"There you go," I heard Rick say. "Make her your whore."

And then someone was licking my asshole. I writhed, trying to concentrate on the hard cock I was swallowing instead of the tongues working my hot holes.

So I was finished with the no hands thing, unless my master told me differently. I got one hand on the black guy's thick shaft, and the other I worked past his balls till I was rubbing his asshole with my thumb. He squatted a little to give my finger more room, and I slid my thumb into his butt. He moaned and stopped licking my cunt.

I worked the head of his cock in my mouth, slobbering everywhere, stroked his thick shaft, and fingered his asshole, while someone was eating my tight little butt. This was too much for the black guy. His balls pulled closer to his body, and the head of his cock swelled. I took him in my mouth just in time to swallow his load as his throbbing cock sent gouts of cum down my throat. I sucked up every drop before I was pulled away and flipped around again.

This time Rick had me, and he wasn't letting me go.

"You're my whore, Anna," he said, kissing me.

Our tongues danced.

"Yes, master," I said when we disengaged.

He held me around the middle with one arm and grabbed my ass with his other hand. Like a pro he maneuvered me so that the head of his massive member was at the entrance of my secret wet spot.

"Are you ready for me, whore?" he hissed.

"Ready and waiting, master," I breathed, and he slid that massive meat in my aching pussy.

I hissed with pleasure, and he slammed his meat all the way to my womb. He was bigger than any of my dildos, and he was filling me up.

"Fuck me, master," I moaned, grinding my hips into him.

"Fuck, you're a tight whore," he gasped, and he got both hands on my ass.

"You're so fucking big, master," I groaned as his cock thrust in and out of my sloppy pussy.

Rick grunted, we kissed, then he walked me back until he was pushing me against the glass window where he pounded me.

"Your husband's right there," he groaned.

I turned my head and saw Vic outside on the grass.

"I don't fucking care, master," I groaned.

Rick pounded me against the glass. I saw Vic turn toward us, and I could almost swear that our eyes met, but I knew he couldn't see me through the one-way glass. Anyway, right then, with that enormous dick splitting my pussy, I didn't care. I didn't care if Vic saw me. I didn't care if anyone saw me, just as long as Rick kept fucking me.

"You like fucking with your husband right there, whore?" he growled into my ear.

"I do, master," I groaned.

"You want to fuck two guys while your husband's right there, whore?" he growled.

"Anything for you, master," I moaned.
"Do you want a dick in that tight ass, whore?" he hissed.

"Please, please, fill me up, master," I moaned. "Treat me like a whore." He pulled me up and carried me like I weighed nothing. I wrapped by legs around him and rode him.

"Grab that bench," he said, without even stopping his thrusting. I was nothing but a fuck toy in his hands.

Full of cock, I was only half aware that the blond guy was pulling over the upholstered bench from the foot of the king-sized bed. He shoved it by the window. Rick carried me to it and lowered himself down so I was on his lap. He lay back.

"Ride me, whore," he ordered, and I did, letting his cock slide in and out its ten-inch length. "Whose cock do you want, Anna?" he asked.

I saw the other two guys standing near the window, waiting. The blond guy was squeezing his cock. The black guy was stroking his. My eyes fixed on the black guy's cock.

Rick saw where I was looking and laughed. "You want the big cock in your ass, whore?" he said.

I blushed, but I looked him in the eyes. "I want the big one in my ass, master," I groaned as I rode his cock.

"You heard the whore," Rick said, and the black guy smiled.

He came around me and leaned over so he could lick my tight butthole.

I was so wet from the cunnilingus that my ass was slick and ready. He worked his tongue inside. That made me buck on Rick's cock like a wild woman.

"You like that, whore?" Rick grunted.

"Yes, master," I groaned.

"Tell him what you want, whore," Rick ordered.

"I want you to fuck my tight ass, please," I groaned, looking back at the black guy.

He came up from my ass and, pulling me by the hair, kissed me. I pulled him tight so our mouths smashed together almost painfully. He grabbed my tits in his strong hands and squeezed them, pinching my hard nipples between his fingers.

I moaned with pleasure as Rick thrust his ten-inch throbbing fuck baton deep inside me.

"You want my big cock, whore?" the black guy growled when we broke apart.

"Yes, please. Fuck my ass, please," I moaned wantonly.

And he grabbed my hips. "If you want that dick, get it in that ass, whore," he ordered.

"Yes, please," I groaned, and I grabbed that two-inch thick man-shaft and pushed the head against my tight, puckered hole.

I worked his cock inside my muscled ring. As soon as the head of his cock breached my two-ringed hole, he savagely thrust himself all the way to the hilt, and Rick did the same. I screamed. It burned, as if my ass was on fire, but the pain was also pleasure, and I didn't want them to stop.

"Fuck me, fuck me, fuck me," I screamed like a mantra.

The black guy was pulling my hair like the reins of a horse as he rode me. Then Rick slapped me, and I snarled at him like an animal. "You like that, whore?" Rick grunted, as the two man pistons pulled out of my holes in unison and then savagely thrust back inside my thrumming body.

It felt like they were splitting me in two, and I screamed again, but now it was true carnal bliss. It was as if my body was a new thing that was discovering that pleasure and pain could intertwine, mingled, to create heaven. The fucking was scratching an itch I never knew I had. Filling a hunger that had never been filled before.

"Use your fucking whore, boys," I screamed, bucking and writhing like the whore I was.

I leaned my body into Rick's, my nipples pressed against his hard chest, and I bit his shoulder.

"I think the bitch's husband heard that," the blond guy said.

I looked up, remembering there was a world outside of my pleasure and pain, and saw Vic outside. He was coming toward the house. He had a curious look on his face. Then the two cocks servicing me were ripped out of my depths and mercilessly thrust back inside, tickling my nerves with agonizing sensation, and I stopped caring about Vic, about anything, but the feelings surging through my body. I was nothing but over-stimulated nerve endings making an electrical storm in my brain.

"We should do something to stop the whore from screaming," the black guy said.

"Get over here." Rick motioned to the blond guy, without stopping his thrusting.

"Fuck me, master," I panted like a dog.

The pressure of the two enormous cocks filling my pussy and asshole was divine torture. The rubbing through the walls of my sex was a revelation of pleasure.

"Suck that dick, whore," Rick ordered, as the blond guy grabbed a handful of my hair and thrust his dick at me.

I sucked the hard cock eagerly and gagged on it. I stopped screaming and started sloppy sucking and grunting. The blond guy had a hand in my hair and was moving my head with his thrusts as he fucked my mouth. The black guy squeezed and pinched my tits. Rick's strong hands were on my hips. And I was connected to all of them through the thrusting dicks and our overriding lust.

Rick and the black guy changed their rhythm so that when one pulled out the other pushed in. The crisscrossed sliding pressure between my vaginal walls and my ass canal was too much. I started to shudder and shake.

"The whore's about to cum," Rick grunted.

"Me, too," the black guy said.

"Fill her up," the blond guy laughed.

I grunted. My mouth was too full to demand their cum, but my body did my demanding. I sucked the cock all the way down my throat, and my pussy and ass tightened. I was going to squeeze the cum out of them.

I wanted it.

I needed it.

The blond guy came first, shooting what felt like gallons of cum down my throat. I sucked and suck up every last drop. Then my orgasm— multi-gasms—took me like a cum tide. My pussy, my ass, my body convulsed as ecstasy crackled between the points of pleasure and careened from head to toe.

Then the black guy slammed his huge dick all the way up my asshole, and I felt the hot cum shoot into me like hot liquid pleasure. Then Rick grabbed me by the hair and pulled me off the dick I was still sucking and kissed me, just as he shot his load into my waiting pussy.

We kissed as the two dicks worked in and out of my holes in slow motion. My body shuddered with every movement.

It felt endless.

Then it was done, and they pulled out of me.

My body ached and throbbed without the dicks. It felt like I was missing something. I wanted more but, with the dicks not controlling me, I knew it was time to end this.

"You boys should go," I said, lying on Rick's broad chest and panting.

"Probably," Rick said.

And we untangled. I sat on the bench while they pulled on their shorts. I looked at their beautiful bodies and gently fingered my tortured pussy.

"It looks like you want more, Anna," Rick said, grinning, and his cock was hard again.

My pussy ached, but it wanted more, and so did I.

"I do, but there's no time," I said.

Outside the window it looked like the yard party was winding down. "Too bad," the black guy said, and he smiled.

That made my pulse go. He was as handsome as Rick, and his dick was beautiful.

"Maybe we can give you a little something before we go," the blond guy said, stroking his cock.

"Like what?" I asked, looking at those hard dicks.

They walked toward me. I lay back, with my feet up on the bench, arching my back and rubbing my body.

"Show us how beautiful you are, Anna," Rick said, standing over me.

I rubbed my hands up and down my body and moved my body in the ways I knew they would like, arching my back and opening my legs. They stared and stroked their cocks. I sucked my finger.

"You like this body?" I moaned.

They answered by stroking their cocks faster.

"You like using this body as your fuck toy?" I asked.

The three young men beat their cocks, their balls bouncing, and their eyes full of desire. Then the black guy burst, shooting cum on my stomach. I rubbed it down to my pussy. The blond guy came on my tits, and I rubbed his cum around. Then Rick—he would always cum last—shot his load in my face. I licked and slurped his seed.

Now it was over.

They left, but not before we made another 'date'.

"Next time you'll be my three whores," I told them.

"Anything you want, master," Rick said, and we kissed.

I couldn't wait.

~ ~ ~

Bad Girl Good Cops

The room was tiny. The walls were bare cinderblock painted white. The door was metal, closed and locked. The floor was industrial tile. There was a TV on a rolling stand in one corner, a white board on the wall, blank, a filing cabinet behind her, a cheap fold-up table in the middle of the room, and the fold-up chair she was sitting in. The chair was metal. It was cold, and having it press against her bare pussy was driving her crazy.

She wiggled. Crossed her legs. Uncrossed her legs. If she could just get rid of this itch between her legs, then maybe she could think straight. She gulped and started to slip her hand under the table.

She stopped and looked up. There was a camera in a corner of the ceiling. It had a red light—the all-seeing eye. They were watching her. She was certain. She stuck out her lower lip as if she was going to cry. She didn't have to fake the quiver. She actually might start crying.

What was she doing? Was she really this stupid? OMG, if her daddy ever found out about this, she was a goner.

No, no, she couldn't think about that. It was too late to undo what was already done. She took a quivering breath and pulled at the hem of her tank. She couldn't keep her hands still, not with that persistent itch demanding attention.

Scratch me, the itch said.

Rub me, the itch said.

But she was so scared.

Maybe she just needed to tell them who she was and end this right now before things got any worse.

And it could get worse.

No, she wouldn't do that.

But she had to do something. How long were they going to make her wait before they told her what they were going to do with her? To her? Her stomach jumped like a jellybean. That just made the itch worse.

There's probably something psychologically wrong with me, she thought. *Kelpto, nympho, or some kind of thing that ends in an 'o.'*

She looked up at the camera and casually slipped her hand under the table. Her stomach flip-flopped like she was on a rollercoaster. There was no way they could see what she was doing under the table. What if they could? That made the itch worse. She touched the inside of her right leg. The touch gave her goose bumps. She brushed her nails over her smooth skin, up her leg, up, up, up toward the itch. Oh, it was so bad. Her little clit needed attention, but would she go farther here, with them watching?

They can't see, she told herself.

Her fingers slipped farther up her thigh. She spread her legs. Bad girl! They couldn't see what she was doing, but they could see enough to guess. They were most likely recording her. She slid her fingers into the deep hollow of her inner thigh.

She stopped breathing.

She pressed the edge of her thumb against her outer folds.

She bit her lip.

There wasn't anything to see. She wasn't doing anything, just touching her leg.

She slipped her fingers under her butt and squeezed. The pressure against her anxious mound made her gasp. She rocked forward. Her wrist pressed into her pussy. She was so wet. If they left her in here much longer, she'd make a mess.

She should stop. She was going to make things worse.

She rocked back and then forward.

I'm not beating off in the security room of an S-Mart, she told herself, wiggling her crouch so the bone in her wrist rubbed her clit just right. *I'm just sitting down,* she told herself, while she shifted her ass to rub her pussy against the chair.

**

"You sure got here fast, officer... uh...?" Sam said.

"Bowens. And he's Cooper," the officer said.

They were in the security room. It wasn't any larger than a walk-in closet. There was a counter against the wall and chairs pushed under it. On shelves above the counter was a bank of security monitors. The three men were watching the monitor showing the girl.

"Who called you?" Sam asked. "We just now grabbed her."

Sam Weber had been the head of the store's Loss Prevention for two years, and the cops had never shown up this fast when they caught a shoplifter.

"We were in the store when it happened," Bowens said.

"We saw the whole thing," Cooper said.

Sam nodded.

The security room felt cramped with three men in it, especially since the two officers were the size of linebackers from a pro-football team. Bowens was the taller of the two, six three at least. He was black, clean cut, with striking hazel eyes. He was watching the camera intently.

Cooper was a little shorter, but wider. He had sandy blond hair and was very fair. He looked like a farm boy who had just walked out of the cornfield.

"What exactly did she steal?" Cooper asked.

Sam pointed to the pile on the counter. Cooper plucked something up and held it out.

"Tiny," he said, holding up the bright red thong.

"She had thirty of them in her purse," Sam said.

Cooper whistled. "Quite a haul," he said.

"Have you searched her?" Bowens asked, not looking away from the monitor.

"For what?" Sam said. "I mean, you see how she's dressed. Where's she going to hide something in that outfit?"

"They have ways," Cooper said.

Bowens nodded.

"I'm going to have a look," Bowens said. "Is that room locked?"

Sam nodded.

"I think it's against State law for store security to lock someone up," Cooper said.

Sam turned red. "It's just you came so fast..." he stammered.

"Give me the keys," Bowens said.

"Sure," Sam said, holding out a key on a ring full of keys.

"Get everything settled," Bowens said to Cooper.

"Settled?" Sam said.

Bowens didn't answer. He took the keys and left the room.

Cooper looked at Sam. "We'll be taking her off your hands," he said.

"Taking her off our hands?" Sam said. "Store policy is to not press charges if the merchandise is less than a hundred dollars, especially if it's recovered. There's some paperwork to sign saying she'll never come back in the store, but that's it."

Cooper nodded, but he wasn't paying attention. He was looking at the monitor. Bowens had just opened the door and was entering the room.

The girl looked up. She was strikingly beautiful. Her eyes got wide when she saw Bowens. He stepped inside and closed the door behind him. He was saying something, but the monitor didn't have sound. The girl shook her head. Her long pigtails bounced.

Bowens gestured with his hand. He was nodding. The girl was biting her lip. She nodded and slowly stood up.

"What's he doing?" Sam said.

"His job," Cooper growled.

Sam shut up.

On the monitor, Bowens was turning the girl toward the door. He was behind her. She was tiny, with a tight little body. Her short tank left a sliver of skin showing off her back dimples. Her mini skirt was hardly long enough to cover a postage stamp. Bowens stood to the side of her, as if he wanted them to see what he was doing. He ran his hands down her arms and around to her breasts.

"I'm not sure about this," Sam said. He was sweating.

Cooper nodded. "I'm sure," he said. "Don't you worry, we'll take it from here."

She stood with her hands against the door. Her legs spread out.

"Don't move," Officer Bowens said.

He was standing next to her. He reached out and grabbed both her wrists. His hands closed around them like she was a toy.

"Why does a pretty girl like you wear so much make-up?" he asked. Her full lips were crimson red. Her eyes were lined with thick black liner and accented with blue eyeshadow. "It makes you look like a slut. Are you a slut?"

"Maybe," she whispered.

Her heart was thumping.

"Really?" he said. "A thief and a slut?"

He ran his hands down her arms, over her elbows, across her biceps, around her shoulders. She held her breath. That tickle flared. His hands were strong. She gasped when he slid them around her side and under her breasts.

"Have to make certain you're not hiding anything," he said, squeezing. She swallowed, bit her lip, and closed her eyes. Her hard nipples were caught between his fingers, and he was pinching, just hard enough to send bolts of pleasure through her body. She squirmed.

"Nothing there," he said. "Well, that's not true. There's a surprising amount there, for someone so small." He squeezed her breasts. "But nothing hidden."

She couldn't help the moan that slipped past her lips.

He hummed and ran his hands slowly down her sides. He lingered on her hips, his thumbs rubbing the dimples on her lower back.

"Such a tiny waist," he said, his voice coming out in a throaty breath.

She gulped.

"Does your boyfriend hold your hips like this when you fuck him?" he asked.

She swallowed.

"I don't have a boyfriend," she whispered.

"I find that hard to believe," he said. "With a tight little body like this, they should be lining up. Don't you like boys?"

"I like boys," she said, shifting her weight from one leg to the other.
"What's your name?" he asked, his hands creeping down her body.

"Chloe," she whispered.

He kneeled behind her, running both hands down her left leg. She spread her legs farther apart and stuck out her butt.

"Listen, Chloe," he said. "We're going to take you down to the station."
She shivered.

His hands slid over her knee-high sock to her ankle. Then he started to back up. He went over her knee, up her thigh, under her skirt, and all the way up to her mound. His hand brushed against her, and she jumped like she was shocked.

"It's ok, Chloe," he said, switching to her other leg.

He rubbed his hand on her inner thigh, while he grabbed her ass. "This is just routine," he said.

She couldn't help it when her back arched. She leaned into the door, her cheek pressed against the cold metal. She licked her lips. The tips of her nipples were brushing the door, and it felt like someone rubbing sandpaper over the sensitive points.

"Yes, sir," she moaned. "I won't resist."

"I know you won't, Chloe," he said, his hands leaving her inner thigh and running down her leg.

Chloe groaned and shifted her hips back and forth.

"You have an amazing body, Chloe," Bowens said.

She shivered.

Someone knocked. Bowens stood up.

"Ok, Chloe," he said. "You're clean."

She stood back, flushed and breathing hard. He was grinning. The bulge in his pants was obvious, and she couldn't take her eyes off it. He opened the door. Officer Cooper was there.

"Are we ready?" Cooper said.

"Very ready," Bowens said.

They handcuffed her, cuffs in front. She looked down, her long, blond pigtails nearly touching the cuffs. She let out a shuddering sigh. It was too late now. There was no going back.

"Are cuffs really necessary?" Sam asked. He looked nervous. "Maybe we should talk to the store manager."

"Are you telling us how to do our job?" Bowens asked. His voice was low and dangerous.

Sam flushed and shook his head. "No, no," he said.

"I think we're finished here," Cooper said.

Bowens nodded.

"Don't you need a statement or something?" Sam asked.

Bowens and Cooper looked at him. He swallowed his tongue.

"Let's go, Chloe," Bowens said.

She looked down, nodded, and walked out past Sam. Bowens followed her, Cooper coming behind. They walked through the store. Customers couldn't help but notice the tiny girl, followed by the two huge cops.

Chloe's face burned under the staring, judgmental eyes. Sunday morning, and these bible thumpers just out of church. She knew they were looking her up and down, from the handcuffs, to her hard nipples pressing through the white tank top and her ass hanging out of the mini skirt. They'd condemn her here, and then run home to jerk off thinking about her. Hypocrites. God, she hated them.

An old, blue-haired biddy pointed. Her husband gawked. Chloe pulled down on her tank so it stretched, making her hard nipples pop out. The old man gaped. She grinned. The biddy slapped him. He was making apologetic noises, but he'd be fapping later and imagining her perky little tits when stroked his cock.

She wondered how many of the guys staring would be running to the bathroom to jerk off right after they left. Pervs.

The three of them left the store.

"Thanks, and come again," the stupid greeter said.

Thanks and come again? She was in handcuffs. What was that nimrod thinking?

The patrol car was parked in front of the store. Bowens went to the driver's side. Cooper took her to the passenger side door. He opened it.

"Watch your head," he said, helping her in by putting a hand on her head and his other meaty hand on her ass.

He grabbed a handful and squeezed her ass cheek. She slid into back seat. He leaned in after her, leering at her long legs.

"You ok back there?" he said.

"I'm fine," she said.

"Great," he said, and he slammed the door.

**

They drove down the main street of the cowpoke town. It was quiet. Sundays kept the folks in for church and football. Chloe was trying not to cry. If she looked up, she'd see Bowens's and Cooper's eyes reflected in their mirror.

"What's going to happen to me?" she asked, without looking up.

"You're in some trouble, that's for sure," Bowens said.

"That's right," Cooper agreed.

"I didn't mean to do anything wrong," she said.

"I guess you though they wouldn't care if you helped yourself," Cooper laughed.

"I only took what I needed," she said.

"Right," Bowens said.

The car pulled to a stop at the town's one stoplight in front of the City Hall.

"It's true," she said, and she slid around until she was on her knees facing the back of the car. "It's just that I don't have any panties to cover my little ass," she said, bending over so the skirt rode up her back.

44

Both cops looked back and saw her pale little ass highlighted by tan lines. She arched her back and rolled her hips.

"My poor little pussy," she moaned. "Was it so wrong to want to cover it?"

"Fuck," Cooper gulped.

She pushed her ass toward the front seat.

"Am I really such a bad girl for wanting to cover my pussy?" she said. "If I am, then I should be punished. You should punish me and my little pussy."

"Damn," Bowens said. With his eyes on the rear-view mirror, he turned the patrol car into the alley between City Hall and The Freemont hotel. Halfway down, he stopped the car.

"Are we there?" Chloe asked, wiggling her butt.

"I think we might take care of this a different way," Bowens said.

"Something just between us," Cooper said.

"A more suitable punishment," Bowens said.

They both got out. Bowens opened one back door, Cooper the other. Chloe slid on all fours in the back seat. She was facing Bowens, and her ass was pointing toward Cooper.

"What kind of punishment?" she asked.

Bowens stood in the door, looking down at her. Cooper reached in the patrol car. He flipped up her skirt and exposed her ass. She licked her lips. Bowens's hands dropped to his belt buckle.

"I think if you're a good girl, we can work something out," he said, unbuckling his belt.

"But I am a bad girl," Chloe purred.

"Bad girls need to be spanked," Cooper said, and he slapped her white ass.

"Oh, yes," Chloe hissed. "I'm so bad." And she lifted up her ass.

Cooper slapped it again, leaving a red hand mark. She moaned. Bowens was undoing his zipper.

"How bad are you?" Bowens asked. "Bad enough for this?" And he pulled out his huge, hard cock.

Chloe bit her lip and stared at the throbbing member. It was dark, with a pink head. She gulped.

"Are you going to use that to punish me?" she mumbled.

He grinned. "That's right, bad girl," he said.

She leaned forward. She was trembling. "I've never seen something so big," she said, kissing the tip.

"Is it too much for you?" Bowens grunted.

"No," she said, and she opened her mouth as wide as she could, taking in the head.

He groaned, and Cooper slapped her ass. She shuddered.

"I think I want a taste of that ass," Cooper said.

He grabbed her hips and leaned into the car, licking her ass. She groaned as she sucked on the big cock. She pulled off the head, slurping.

"Maybe you want to take these off," she said, gangling the cuffs.

"Bad girls need cuffs," Bowens said. He reached down, grabbed the cuffs, and pulled them up so she was hanging out the car by her arms. She panted. Cooper licked her asshole. She moaned. He reached around her and pawed her breasts.

"Punish me," she moaned.

"Suck my dick, slut," Bowens said, pulling up her arms and pushing his cock toward her mouth.

She licked the head. He grabbed the shaft of his huge cock and slapped her face. She opened her mouth, and he pushed his cock over her lips. She licked.

Cooper had worked his tongue to her pussy, and he was running the tip through her folds. She squirmed. Bowens shoved his cock in her mouth. She took him and gagged on his length.

"This one's a really bad girl," Bowens groaned.

"She's got a great little pussy," Cooper said. "I need to fuck it."

She moaned around the thick cock.

"Go ahead," Bowens said. "She wants it. Don't you, Chloe?"

She let the big cock slide out of her throat. "Yes, fuck me," she groaned, and she took the cock back in her mouth.

Cooper undid his pants and crawled into the car. He pulled his cock out of his shorts. It was as big as Bowens's. He slid the head up and down on her slit. She moaned and slurped.

"She's so damn wet," Cooper said, and he slid his cock inside her. "Fuck, she's tight." He went slowly.

She pulled back from Bowens's massive dick. "Fuck me," she growled.

Cooper grabbed her hips and slid out of her wet pussy, then went right back in. She arched her back, as he slid to the hilt. He slid back out and slowly slid back in. She rode him, grinding her ass against him.

"Oh, Lordy. Oh, Lordy," she moaned.

Cooper ran his thumb over her asshole. She gasped. "Your ass is virgin?" he asked, laughing.

"Yes," she mewed.

"Lube that ass up for me," Bowens said, and he grabbed her head and shoved his cock toward her mouth.

She took in his cock, just as Cooper squeezed a glob of lube on her ass, then he slid his thick thumb in her butt, in and out. She bucked.

Then they were both fucking her. Cooper's cock sliding in and out of her tight cunt, his thumb in her ass, and Bowens fucking her face with his huge cock. She couldn't take it. She was so full. It felt so great. She writhed, gagged, and moaned.

Then she came, ecstasy exploding from her.

"You should feel that ass squeezing," Cooper said. "It's eager."

Bowens only grunted and shot his load down her throat. She choked and swallowed his gushing sperm. He pulled out, still throbbing, and shot cum all over her face. His thick seed dripped, and she licked up what she could. Then she felt Cooper stiffen as he filled her pussy with his seed.

"Fuck, that was great," she panted, and she licked the head of Bowens's cock.

"You are a bad girl," he moaned.

Cooper smacked her ass. She grinned. "That I am," she said.

"Let's get these off you," Bowens said, undoing the handcuffs. He tossed them on the patrol car floor.

"Is that all the punishment I get?" she asked, grinning.

"I don't think so," he growled. He reached into the car and pulled her out.

She let out a little scream. He was so strong. He pulled her into his chest. She wrapped her arms around him, and they kissed.

"Fuck, someone's going to see," Cooper said.

"All the fuckers are at church," Chloe said, pulling back.

"Let's give them something to see," Bowens said, carrying her to the front of the car.

Holding her up, he spun her around until her back was against his broad chest. She leaned her head back into him.

"What are you planning?" she cooed.

"I want that tight ass," he said, grabbing her around the middle with one hand and pulling her tank top over her head with the other.

She grabbed her bare tits and squeezed. "Fuck that ass," she moaned.

He sat on the hood and lowered her onto his cock. She leaned over and grabbed the shaft.

"Oh, my, it's so thick," she moaned, pressing the head of his cock against her brown flower.

"Too big for you, bad girl?" he growled.

"No way," she said, wiggling her butt.

He lowered her down and slowly slid through her tight twin rings.

She moaned. "You're ripping me in two, big boy," she hissed. "But it feels so fucking good."

Cooper came around the car. He kneeled and licked her pussy. She grabbed his hair.

"Lick it, bitch," she moaned.

Bowens lifted her up, sliding just a little out of her ass, then he let her down, sliding back in. She reached back and grabbed his head. Cooper kept licking her pussy. Bowens slowly slid inside her ass.

"Oh, Lordy, that feels so fucking good," she moaned when his cock was buried to the hilt.

"You're so damn tight, bad girl," Bowens moaned.

"Let's fill that pussy, too," Cooper said, and he pressed the head of his hard cock against her wet slit.

"Go slow," she breathed.

Her eyes were closed. She was concentrating on the mix of pleasure and pain of having a nine-inch long cock shoved to the hilt in her butt.

"The bad girl wants it slow, eh?" Cooper whispered, sliding his cock inside her wet pussy.

She screamed with pleasure when he slid deep. "Fuck yes!"

Cooper pulled his slick cock back out and slid it back in. Bowens didn't move his cock in her ass. He stayed planted, while Cooper slowly fucked her pussy.

"Fill me up," she moaned.

Cooper grabbed her tits and squeezed. Bowens had his hands on her ass. She wanted more.

"Faster, you bastards," she moaned.

Cooper moved faster.

"Fuck, fuck, fuck," she screamed.

A car went by the alley. They didn't even look.

Bowens shifted his cock out and back in. That was a new feeling. She could feel the two cocks through the thin wall of skin. They moved in unison, one out and one in. They pressed their bodies into her, smashing her between them. She was the meat in their sandwich. The muscles in her ass and pussy contracted. She moaned with animal pleasure.

"Faster," she growled.

She had never felt this full.

Then they were both just thrusting inside her. The feeling was so intense, she thought she was going to hyperventilate. Her ass was tightening like one continuous orgasm. Then she burst, and the rapturous wave took her. She didn't even feel when they came. She hardly felt when Bowens put her in the back of the car.

**

Bowens parked on the side of the S-Mart's parking lot, next to the garden center, near the Lube Express. There was only one other car in this part of the parking lot. It was a bright red 2015 Camaro, with a black racing stripe, a hood scoop, smoked windows, and rally wheels.

"We're here," he said.

Chloe stretched in the back seat and got up. She looked around. There wasn't a soul in sight.

"Thanks," she said, grabbing her purse from the floor of the car.

The two cops got out. Cooper opened her door. She slid out of the car and tiptoed to give him a kiss on the cheek. He blushed.

"You ok to drive?" Cooper asked.

She unhooked the blond wig and threw it in the back seat of the patrol car. She pulled off the wig cap and let out her dark hair.

"Come on, Herald," she said, squeezing his arm. "We fucked, we didn't drink."

His blush deepened.

"Throw the wig away for me, will you?" she said to Bowens.

"You don't think you'll need it again?" he asked, smiling.

"If we do this again, we won't do it like this," she said. "This was a one time thing."

"A risky thing," he said. "What happens if the sheriff hears about it?"

"If my daddy hears about any of this," she said, grinning, "he'll shoot both of you and ground me forever."

"Fuck, that's no joke," Cooper said, looking suddenly pale.

"Don't worry, it'll be fine," she said, walking to the Camaro. "I'm not going to tell him."

"That's some birthday present," Bowens said, eyeing the car.

"Yeah, well, it's not as good as the one you guys just gave me," she said, slipping into the car.

"Happy eighteenth," he said.

"Thanks," she said, and she slammed the door.

They watched her drive away.

~~~

ELEVATOR TO THE TOP

Jan Johnson read the email for the hundredth time. Certain words jumped out at her, 'restructuring' 'workforce', 'streamlined organization', 'bold future', and 'parting ways'.

"The dick is firing me," she exclaimed.

There was no one in the office to hear her. She stood up, threw the door open, and stomped out. She went down to the bank of elevators. She stepped into an open elevator and swiped her key card. The top floor was key card protected. Only associates of Sterling Inc. rated access to the inner sanctum. The scanner turned red, and 'Rejected' flashed on the screen.

"He cancelled my card. The total dick!" she spat.

Angry, she stomped out of the elevator and paced down the hall, hardly noticing the eyes that followed her swaying progress.

Jan Johnson was thirty-one. She was five feet seven inches tall and slender, with long brown hair, wide-set brown eyes, a generous mouth, a straight nose, and determined chin. She wore navy dress pants, a white dress shirt, and black heels. She wasn't a model but she was, as her mother had once told her, well-constructed, and, if not beautiful, then pretty the way normal people are pretty. But there was no denying that she had an air about her that drew attention, and it wasn't unusual for eyes to follow her well-proportioned posterior. Normally she would have noticed the attention and, depending on her mood, she might have either been gratified by it or irritated. Today she was too distracted to notice it. Today she was too angry to care.

Suddenly, she stopped pacing. An idea had come to her. She wheeled on her heels, stalked back to the elevators, got inside one, and went down. She got out in the lobby and glanced at her wristwatch. 1:40.

She looked around and saw a group of young men in dark suits. They resembled each other so closely they might as well have been clones. They were junior associates in training, and they happened to be exactly what she needed. She strode toward them and walked behind them.

They went toward the elevators, but had to wait because the first one was taken by two large men moving a filing cabinet on a furniture dolly. Stewing with anger, Jan studied the men. One of them was tall and had a warm caramel-hued skin and incredibly broad shoulders that tapered down to a lean waist. The other man was slightly shorter and fair. Watching his massive biceps flex and his muscular thighs strain against his work pants as he steadied the filing cabinet, Jan couldn't help but compare him to the suit-wearing clones around her.

The comparison wasn't kind to the young associates.

But Jan didn't have time to admire the male physique. She had something to take care of with Mitch Sterling, the CEO of Sterling Industries.

When the next elevator opened, the gaggle of suits piled in, and Jan slipped in with them. One of the suits swiped his key card, the elevator doors closed, and started whirling toward the top floor. Apart from a few sporadic sidelong glances directed at her breasts or her butt, they hardly looked at her. They all knew who she was and none of them would question her right to be on the top floor.

Jan stomped past the secretary without affording her even a glance.

"Excuse me, you can't go in there…" Mitch Sterling's 'fembot' cried out, getting up from her chair and running after Jan.

But Jan ignored her. She opened the door and strode into the lavish office.

Mitch Sterling looked up from behind his desk. He didn't look surprised.

"Jan," he said by way of greeting, and he smiled his devilish smile.

Jan stopped in front of his desk and looked daggers at him. She couldn't believe she once thought he was something special.

Mitch Sterling, the head of a fortune five hundred company that he built by himself right out of business school, was only thirty-nine. He was athletic.

"I could have been an Olympic swimmer, but business was my calling," he had told Fortune Magazine for the interview in the issue dedicated to him.

And he wasn't lying. He was a physical specimen, standing six feet four inches tall, and he had the looks to match, strong features, ocean blue eyes, and curly locks that were maybe a little unconventionally long for a CEO, but who would dare cut them?

In short, Mitch Sterling was perfect, except for one thing: he was a complete and utter dick!

"You fired me and I would love to hear why," Jan barked.

Mitch Sterling pursed his lips in an expression that was meant to be sympathy, or understanding—or so she assumed—but he managed to look smugger than ever.

"Unfortunately, Ms. Johnson, we're streamlining," he said with a shrug. "You've been a valuable employee and it'll be hard to let you go, but I know you'll have no trouble finding a similar position someplace else."

She snorted. "You must be joking if you think I buy your bullshit. Did you practice this speech in the mirror, or did your lawyer write it for you?"

He grinned, and his eyes sparkled.

"This is because I said no to your advances, isn't it?" she snapped.

A week before, Mitch Sterling had paid her a visit to her office. It hadn't been a scheduled meeting, she had been working late, and it had been quite a surprise for Jan when he locked the door behind him. He had been in black trousers and one of his tailored white dress shirts. He had been flushed, and she had thought he might have been drinking.

"Jan," he had said, "you've been with the company for a year and in that time I've had my eyes on you."

That hadn't been a surprise. She knew he had been watching her. At first, she had been excited by his interest, but then there had been the incident at the company pool. She had been swimming laps before work and so had he. When she got out of the pool, he had greeted her normally enough but the erection in his speedo had been painfully obvious. She had felt so uncomfortable that she had run. Ever since, she had avoided him as best she could. Jan was all too aware of Mitch Ster-

58

ling's reputation and she didn't want to be one of his conquests. Being pinned to that trophy board could ruin her career, and she had worked too hard to get where she was.

Then there had been that time in her office.

"Here's the thing, Jan. I think we could do great things together," he had said.

"I hope I can make a difference at Sterling," she had said, hoping to steer the conversation toward work.

But Mitch Sterling hadn't come with the intention to talk about work and he hadn't beaten around the bush.

"You can help Sterling with this right now," he had said, and then he had pulled out his erect penis from his pants.

Jan had gotten up from behind her desk and run out of her office. She had taken a week sick leave after that embarrassing incident, and when she returned today she found out he fired her.

"Jan," Mitch Sterling said, getting up and slowly coming around the desk, "I assure you it's nothing personal. It's a company decision. Reorganization and all that. Layoffs happen all the time as you well know."

He smiled benevolently at her.

Her brow furrowed in a frown.

"How many other people beside myself are being reorganized?" she asked.

"At the moment, you're the only one, I'm afraid," he said candidly.

"Do you think you can get away with this?" she snapped.

"Get away with what, Jan?" he asked, looking grave, but his eyes were still dancing with delight.

He was enjoying this.

"You can't fire someone for not sucking your dick," she said bluntly.

"Ah. That's where you're wrong. I can fire anyone I like," he said. "It's my company after all."

"I'll sue," she said.

"Will you?" he said. "A friendly word of advice before you do that. It'll be your word against mine, and I have the money to make sure my word is the one that is heard."

"You pompous dick," she snarled.

"Insulting me won't help your situation," he said. He stepped closer and put his hands on her shoulders. "I honestly think this is for the best. The sad fact is that you're not cut out for Sterling. You're not a team player."

Jan looked up at him. "What if I was a team player?" she asked.

He stared into her eyes for a few silent seconds that seemed like hours, then his grin grew even wider.

"If you prove to me that you can take one for the team, then perhaps the decision can be revoked," he said, and he reached out and undid one of her shirt buttons.

Jan bit her lip. This was her career that he was so cavalierly talking about. If she got fired from Sterling Industries, she knew she could get another job but not one as good. And if Mitch Sterling got it into his head to blackball her, she'd be finished at any major company. She'd be toxic.

He undid another button, and her shirt opened as her bra pushed her cleavage out. Mitch Sterling raised his eyebrows in approval as he looked down at her cleavage.

Blackballed or just balled, she thought.

"Fine," she said. "I can take one for the team."

"That's what we like to hear at Sterling," Mitch Sterling said, clapping. "And there's no time like the present, wouldn't you agree?"

He undid his belt, opened his trousers, and pulled out his swelling cock.

Jan looked down at it. It was just a cock, and what had a cock, any cock, ever done to her? It was its master that was the real dick. The cock just wanted a little attention, a little love, a little caress, and a kiss. That wasn't too much to do to keep her job.

Ten minutes of work. She had done worse.

Mitch Sterling looked at her. His expression said, 'Get on with it.'

Jan got on her knees in front of him and put a hand on his hard shaft. He put a hand on her head. The tip of his cock glistened with pre-cum. She licked it. Mitch Sterling was a complete dick, but his cum wasn't bitter. It was earthy and almost sweet.

"That's it, Jan," he said, looking down at her.

She held his eyes, swirling her tongue around his swollen head.

"Yes," he moaned, as she took him in her mouth. "You know you want it."

She pulled back. He looked at her. She got up and wiped her mouth.

"No," she said decisively.

"I beg your pardon?" he said.

"I'll suck your cock, if that's what it takes, but I'm not going to pretend I want it. That's just asking too much from me."

"What?" he said, looking baffled.

"You might be god's gift to humanity," she said, "but that doesn't mean I want to suck your cock."

"You're a lesbian, is that your problem?" he said.

She laughed. "I'm not a lesbian," she said.

"You must be frigid," he said. "That's what everyone says."

"Everyone says I'm frigid?" she spluttered.

He shrugged noncommittally.

"I'm not frigid," she growled.

"Then I really fail to see what your problem is," he said.

"You're really dense, aren't you? The problem is that I don't want to suck your dick," she said.

"Then you're fired," he said.

"Fine," she said, and she stomped out of his office. "Your boss needs you to suck his dick," she growled at the 'fembot' as she passed by her desk.

**

The elevator door was starting to close. Jan ran toward it and managed to stop it from closing. The elevator opened, and, to her surprise, she saw the two men she had noticed earlier in the lobby. Their dolly was empty. Without hesitation Jan stepped inside the elevator. She wasn't about to stand around and wait for another one.

She turned to face the door. She didn't want them to see her crying. She stabbed the 'L' for lobby, even though it was already lit, and the door closed at last and the elevator started to go down.

She wasn't crying because she was sad. She was crying because she was pissed. Mitch Sterling had called her frigid because she hadn't wanted to suck his dick, and what else had he said? That they all thought she was frigid.

Who was all?

Had all the associates discussed her sex life?

Maybe the topic of whom she fucked was on the board's weekly agenda. The inside of the elevator was mirrored, and she could see the two men behind her looking at her. Then the two shared a look. Suddenly, she turned to face them.

"Do I look frigid to you?" she asked, looking at the one with the caramel complexion.

His eyes ran slowly up and down her body, as if he was making a careful judgment.

"No, you don't look frigid," he said thoughtfully, staring down into her cleavage.

Her shirt was still half open. Jan rolled her eyes.

"It's all about tits with you men, isn't it?" she said, wiggling her chest.

"Not all," the dark man said, "but tits help."

"What about you?" Jan asked, turning to the other man.

He looked at her half-heartedly, then looked away.

"William doesn't like elevators," the dark man explained.

"Oh, I'm sorry," Jan said, feeling suddenly embarrassed.

"He'll be ok as long as we don't break down," the dark man said. "I'm Jacob, by the way."

"Um, yeah, nice to meet you," she said, feeling suddenly shy under his forward stare.

She turned her back to the men and wrapped her arms around her.

"If it's any consolation," Jacob said from behind her, "you've got a great butt, too."

Jan's cheeks were aflame.

"Thanks," she said, feeling incredibly embarrassed and, to her surprise, surprisingly hot.

Jacob was mouthwatering. He wasn't the kind of guy who had to force himself on anyone. She met his dark eyes in the mirror. His look was full of raw carnal desire. It made her shiver.

Then the elevator shook, the light blinked, there was a loud bang, and the elevator came to an abrupt stop.

"What happened? Why aren't we moving?" William asked in obvious distress.

Jacob turned to him. "It's nothing, Will. Relax," he said.

"We're trapped," William moaned. His green eyes looked wild, and sweat beaded on his forehead.

"We're not trapped, Will," Jacob said, his deep voice soothing.

"Then let me out," William said, his voice cracking.

"We'll get out, don't worry," Jacob said, reaching out a hand as if to steady William.

William pushed him away.

"We're trapped," he gasped, looking wildly around the tiny space.

"Will, listen to me, everything will be ok," Jacob said, but William wasn't listening.

He was slowly turning in a circle, and he beat one of his hands repeatedly against his thigh. He was about to lose it.

Jan watched William with growing concern. She didn't like being stuck in the elevator any more than he did, but she wasn't going to let it drive her crazy. She couldn't say the same for William. He looked as if he was under a full moon and about to go full werewolf in the tiny cabin of the elevator.

No way that would be good.

Without thinking, Jan stepped toward him and grabbed his hands.

"Hey," she said, "You're William, aren't you?"

His gaze turned toward her, his wild eyes barely registering her.

"William, look at me," she said. "It's going to be all right. Do you understand?"

He shook his head repeatedly. "We're trapped," he cried, pulling away from her.

Jan held on to his hands. She knew she had to get him under control. She stepped closer to him.

"It's not so bad, Will," she cooed. "You're with a pretty girl. Lots of guys would like to be in here with me."

"Yeah, Will," Jacob agreed. "She's gorgeous."

William looked at her, blinked, then his eyes came to rest on her cleavage.

"How do you like these?" she said, letting go of his hands so she could heft her breasts. "They're nice, huh?" She lifted her chest, squeezing out even more cleavage that the push-up offered.

"I'll say." Jacob whistled.

Jacob was standing close behind her and was looking down over her shoulder. She could feel the heat radiating from his body, and suddenly she became acutely aware of how sexy and how powerfully masculine his body was and her breath caught in her throat.

It had been a long time since she looked at a man simply as a man and not as competition or a colleague. Work had taken up all her time, but not anymore. She didn't want to think about that anymore. And especially not now.

"Don't you like what you see, Will?" Jan said, and she leaned toward him.

William nodded, but he stepped back, his wild eyes darting up and over her. She had to get his attention quickly, or he was going to lose it. She started undoing the rest of the buttons on her shirt. Suddenly she felt strong hands helping her out of her shirt. It was Jacob. She looked at him over her shoulder.

A roguish smile played on his lips. "Just being helpful," he said, taking her shirt.

"Thanks," she said wryly.

She was left in a purple lacy push-up. Feeling confident that the bra displayed her not so modest-sized breasts perfectly, she cupped her chest in her hands and leaned forward toward William.

"What do you think of my bra, Will? Isn't it a lovely bra?" she teased.

"Yeah," William mumbled, ogling the round peaks of her breasts.

She was happy to see that she had finally managed to get his attention, but a second later he looked away. She stepped toward him and pressed her chest against his.

"Don't worry about the elevator, worry about me," she breathed, and she kissed him.

At first, he didn't return her kiss, but when she ran her fingers down his belly to the front of his pants, his attention turned on her, like she was fire and he was about to get burned. Instantly one of his hands fell on her hip and the other landed on the back of her neck. Her hand found a growing bulge in his pants, and she rubbed it.

"There's nothing to worry about, Will, nothing at all," she breathed on his lips when their kiss broke.

William was panting. She kissed his lips lightly and rubbed his erection through his pants.

"How are you feeling, Will? Don't you feel much better?" she cooed.

"Yeah," he said, sounding excited, but not scared. "Much."

Then the elevator rocked.

William gasped, and his erection shriveled visibly. He looked up at the ceiling of the elevator, his eyes wide like a frightened bunny. He started to pull away from Jan, but Jan crushed her lips to his and slipped her legs around his well-muscled thigh. She kissed him frantically, and vigorously humped his leg. There was no time to be gentle. The rubbing made her pussy ache, but she found the sensation curiously rousing. When she felt his cock swelling and his hands slipped around her to cup her ass, she had almost forgotten why she was doing what she was doing.

"There's nothing to worry about, Will, nothing at all," she whispered, slowly grinding herself into his thigh.

"Nothing at all," he breathed, and he kissed her deeply, tangling his eager tongue with hers.

He pulled her to him, pressing her into his hard chest. Then she felt another pair of hands on her back. She turned her head and saw Jacob grinning at her.

"You did a great job," he said.

"You really think so?" she said, smiling, while William kissed her neck and her chest.

Jacob's fingers ran up her back, and, like magic, her purple push-up snapped open. She wiggled out of it, while William kissed her tumbling breasts. She arched her back, pushing her rock-hard nipples toward his skillful mouth. He sucked the sensitive points between his lips, nipping her gently, while Jacob's hands rubbed over her back.

There was so much man touching her, feeling her, having her in this small space that their combined scent was intoxicating her. The myriad of feelings and sensations made her tremble with pleasure, and she felt herself getting all wet.

She ran her hands through William's hair. She was suddenly feeling hot, and clothes became just too much to bear.

"You need to get out of these clothes," she said, clawing at his work shirt.

William shrugged out of his shirt revealing his cut chest and smooth muscled belly. Jan ran her hand over the muscles and a shiver of antic-ipation ran through her, while rough hands slipped around her waist and started opening her pants.

"Let me help you out of your pants," Jacob said, gently biting her bare shoulder.

Jan moaned, arching her back and pressing her bottom into him as he pushed her pants down. Once they were down, she could kick them off.

"You're beautiful," William said, running his hands up her sides and to her full, heavy breasts.

His touch filled her with fire. William ran his fingers over her painfully hard nipples teasing them and making her moan. This was going too far, and she knew it, but she didn't want it to stop. She undid his belt and his pants as the two men touched her, squeezed her, and kissed her. She pushed down William's pants, and her mouth dropped open when his perfect pink hard penis popped out. It was thick and long, but not monstrous. She reached down and took him in her hand.

"Oh my, your cock is Jan-sized," she giggled, stroking his shaft.

"How about this cock?" Jacob said from behind.

She felt Jacob's manhood press into her lower back. She half turned and looked at Jacob's cock. It was a twin in size to William's cock, but Jacob's was darker along the shaft, with a pink head. She reached a hand back to stroke his cock. Now she had both hands full of man. Jacob and William shared a glance. They looked like two cats with a juicy canary between them.

"Who doesn't like elevators, boys?" Jan giggled, rubbing the heads of the two cocks across her smooth skin.

"What elevator?" William said, pulling her to him and kissing her with such want that there was nothing else in the world.

Then there was only kissing and touching.

William's hands ran up and down her body, the touch of his rough palms against her skin making her tingle and writhe, while Jacob's strong hands slid around her body to her breasts. His dark hands gave her breasts a gentle squeeze, and he fingered her pink demanding nipples. Jan had one hand on William's hard cock and was stroking it, and her other hand was wrapped around Jacob's thick thigh, pulling his hard body against her so his thick, insistent cock pressed into the cleft of her butt.

"I feel like a Jan sandwich," she panted, her mouth watering at the display of such manly virility surrounding her.

"That sounds good enough to eat," Jacob said, kissing her shoulders.

"Then why not take a bite?" Jan moaned, pushing her buttocks back into Jacob insistently.

"I will," he growled, and he started kissing down her back.

Jan buried her head in William's chest while she rubbed the head of his cock against her wet slit. Jacob kissed down her back and knelt behind her. He pulled her hard toward him and slid his tongue between her buttocks, while William slowly pushed her head down toward his waiting cock.

"What do you boys have in mind?" she managed to say before her words became a moan as Jacob teased his cock over her brown flower and across her aching pussy.

And then she was bent over, with William's manhood poking toward her, like a man lollipop ready for a sucking. Eagerly, Jan licked his crown, tasting the salty promise of his glistening pre-cum, while Jacob deliciously parted her budding pink folds with the tip of his tongue, sending her into a delirium of pleasure. Her blood pumped as she rode the tidal wave of wild pheromones to places she had never dreamed of before. This was pleasure, given and taken, in its purest form. This was raw desire. This was delight.

Jacob put his hands on her butt, opening her to his explorations and spearing her wet center with this firm, hot tongue, while she slid her lips slowly down William's thick, vein-covered shaft, taking as much of him in her mouth as she could. She had her hands on his hips, and he had his hands tangled in her hair. The only sounds were the slick wet sounds of their bodies and William's low, breathy grunts as Jan fucked him with her mouth.

The mirrored walls of the elevator caught every move, and from the corner of her eye Jan watched it all. It was like seeing another woman, a beautiful, sexual woman, being serviced by two gods of sex, one in front, holding her head, the other behind, holding her ass.

This should be a statue, she thought wildly, as William's long cock touched the back of her throat. Then Jacob's tongue found her swollen clit, and she couldn't do anything but moan with pleasure as sensations sparked through her body, shooting from her pussy like lightning in a storm.

She moaned with William's cock in her mouth. Her body twitched and writhed, her pulse raced maddeningly, and she thought she'd collapse. Before she knew what happened, William lowered himself to the ground and she followed him, ending up on her knees, her lips holding onto his cock like it was a life preserver and she was drowning.

"That's some piece of ass," Jacob said, slapping her rear.

The slap was like connecting jumper cables on a car, and she bucked.

Jacob laughed.

"You like that?" he growled.

"Yes," Jan moaned.

"How about this?" he said, and he positioned himself behind her, ready to mount her.

She could only close her eyes and suck on William's cock as Jacob slid the masthead of his throbbing manhood past her inner lips. He used his fingers to spread her open for his male invasion and, with a single viscous thrust, he buried himself to her hilt.

Her scream was muffled by William's cock in her mouth, but her trembling couldn't be contained. She shook from her curled toes to her clenched lips around William's cock, and she would have slumped to the ground, transformed by the heady mix of pleasure and pain into a quivering mass of jello, if Jacob hadn't held her up with his strong hands clamped to her hips.

"You have to try this tight pussy, Will," Jacob said.

"It can't be better than her mouth," William said, and they high-fived above her.

That was nearly too much for Jan. She watched herself, seeing the length of Jacob's long cock as he slowly pulled out of her wet, dripping pussy, only to slam back into her with a long thrust of his powerful hips. She arched her back to make him go even deeper, and he hit a spot inside her that made her want to howl like a wolf.

"She wants it badly, Will," Jacob grinned, and he slid in and out of her again.

William didn't answer. His eyes were fluttering open and closed, like the wings of a butterfly, as Jan frantically sucked up and down his thick shaft with her plump wet lips while cradling his balls and fingering his tight pleasure hole.

"Fuck me, that's awesome," William groaned, and he pushed Jan's head into his flat belly, burying her nose in his thick, red thatch.

Jacob fingered her butt while her other pink lips clenching around his thick member as he pounded her pussy again and again, his balls exquisitely slapping her clit with every stroke. Then Jacob stopped, his cock buried to the hilt in her dripping pussy. His lack of movement felt like losing something she desperately needed. She pulled back from William's cock.

"Don't stop, not now," she moaned, wiggling her ass.

Jacob didn't move, he only slapped her ass.

"Please! I want more," she groaned, arching her back.

"No. I want you to fuck me," he ordered.

Jan eagerly obliged. She rolled her hips until his cock slid out of her and then thrust back to bring him back inside her.

"That's so good," she moaned, thrusting against him.

Jacob reached around her and his fingertips found her joy button. He started to rub it, not too hard, not too slow, but just right, as if he knew exactly how she liked it.

"Oh, yes, yes, yes!" Jan moaned, as the pressure built inside her sending her higher and higher into ecstasy.

Then William pulled her hair and thrust his cock back into her open mouth. She took him, and she fucked both of them until she felt William's balls pull closer to his body. A second later, he was shooting gushing cum down her throat. She swallowed all of it, relishing the taste of him.

"I'm cumming, baby," Jacob groaned, slamming his cock deeper than ever inside her.

She felt his cum filling her. It felt like gallons, and it triggered her climax. Waves of joy and agony shook her body. The orgasm took her, and she felt her body squeezing Jacob's cock for every drop of his man juice. But Jacob pulled out of her dripping pussy, and he was still shooting. In the mirror she saw him shooting ropes and ropes of hot juice over her butt and back.

"That's some great fucking," he groaned, his body shaking with every shot.

Then he collapsed on her back, and she leaned into William. They lay like that, awkwardly and uncomfortably, but none of them was willing to move. It was too perfect. Jan between their virile forms, their half hard cocks pressed into her, hot cum dripping from her, strong hands holding her.

She kissed William, and turning, she kissed Jacob, his tongue twirling around hers, her taste still on his lips. And then she felt something pressing into her back.

"Fuck, what's that?" she panted, breaking from Jacob's lips. "Are you hard again?"

Jacob grinned and squeezed her ass.

"Isn't everyone?" William said, pinching her nipples.

"What do you want from me now?" Jan said, grinning.

"I want to try that tight pussy," William said, pulling Jan up on his lap. She got up on her knees and reached between her legs to aim his manly harpoon at its wet, pink target. She slid down on him, taking him in. The sensation was exquisite. Jacob rubbed his hand down her back through the hot cum, then he slid his hand down through the cleft of her butt until his cum-slick thumb was pressed against her tight back door.

"Ohh," Jan moaned, as he slipped his thumb through those double rings.

She undulated her hips, feeling the cock and the thumb inside her. William kissed her. Jacob fingered her ass, using more and more of the cum she was covered in to get her ready.

"I want that ass," Jacob breathed into her ear.

His breath sent tingles down her body, and his thumb lit a fire inside her only one thing could quench.

"Yes!" she moaned, leaning into William's chest to give Jacob room to penetrate her from behind.

Jacob slid behind her, and she felt the push of his masthead against her bottom. She held her breath as he slowly entered her.

"It's so tight," he hissed as her rings closed on him.

Jan had never had something so big inside her ass. Her Wallbanger's main shaft was as thick as Jacob, but she had only used that on her pussy, and the second shaft didn't have his girth. With both men's cocks inside her, she felt as if she were being pulled in two.

"Slow," she breathed, as Jacob slid inside her.

William didn't move, but the pressure of Jacob's cock sliding past his with just the thin walls of her body between them made his cock swell, filling Jan even more. When Jacob was all the way inside her, the world stopped moving. There was only the pressure of the two cocks inside her and her thundering heartbeat.

She breathed, and her body adjusted to the girth inside her. She started to move, slowly rocking her hips back and forth. The feeling was divine. She started to move faster. William put his hands on her hips. Jacob's hands were on her shoulders. They found a rhythm. They moved faster, William in and Jacob out. Jacob in and William out.

Jan watched the scene in the mirror. Bodies moving, touching, joining. It was beautiful, and it felt incredible. She felt as if she had been thrown into a sea of ecstasy and was being pounded by waves of rapture. She wasn't sure she could take this much pleasure. The intense feeling of the two cocks sliding in and out of her was driving her insane.

She leaned into William's chest and buried her head in his shoulder. She wrapped her arms around his middle, needing to hold something solid.

"Oh, oh, oh!" was all she could moan.

And then the sensations surged, and she exploded. There was no containing the feeling. She screamed, and her body flushed. She felt hot and cold.

"Yes, yes, yes!" she screamed, throwing her head back.

Wanting more, but not knowing if she could take more.

Suddenly, William stopped moving and his hands closed painfully on her hips. He leaned back, thrusting into her, and she felt his cum gush inside her. A second later, Jacob pulled her down and ground his pelvis into her round butt, shooting his hot load inside her ass.

**

"Can you stand up?" Jacob asked, looking down at her.

"Do you think you're so good that I can't stand after being fucked by you?" Jan said, grinning.

He smirked and held out his hand. She took it.

"How do you feel, Will? Do you think you can handle this elevator ride?" she asked.

William was already dressed, but his shirt was unbuttoned.

"Yeah, I think so," he said.

"I'm happy to hear it," she said, "because I think I'm all fucked out for a while." And she pulled on her panties.

"Who said you were frigid?" Jacob asked, pulling on his pants.

"Some asshole," Jan said, putting on her bra.

She reached down and picked up her pants, and the elevator lurched once and then started moving.

"Oh, great," she said, slipping into her shirt and pants in a hurry. "How do I look?" she asked a little out of breath as she fixed her hair in the mirror.

"Like you ran a marathon," Jacob said, laughing.

Jan shrugged. What did it matter now?

When the elevator doors opened, Mitch Sterling was standing there, looking as smug as he possibly could. Sidney Ward, the company's head lawyer, was close at his side, wearing a dispassionate expression on his face and carrying a very intimidating briefcase.

"Ms. Johnson," Mitch Sterling said. "Sorry about the elevator." Then looking at her more closely, he asked, "Is everything all right?" Then his eyes fell on Jacob and William. "What happened in here?"

"Other than you firing me because I wouldn't fuck you, you mean?" Jan said.

"Yes, about that," Mitch Sterling said. "There are some papers for you to sign."

"It's nothing serious," Sidney Ward assured her, stepping forward.

Jan smiled snidely. "You're afraid I'll sue you," she said.

"Oh no, it's not that," Mitch Sterling said, reaching for her and grabbing her wrist.

"I'm not signing anything," Jan snapped. "And you'll be hearing from my lawyer."

"You don't want to do this, Jan," Mitch Sterling warned her.

Jan looked down at his hand.

"Is this asshole bothering you?" Jacob asked, coming to stand next to her.

"This is none of your business," Mitch Sterling said curtly.

He was standing eye to eye with Jacob.

"If you don't let her go, we'll make it our business," William said, coming to stand on her other side.

Mitch Sterling glared at the two men, and finally he let go of Jan's arm.

"We need to talk about this, Jan," he said.

"No, we don't," she said. "I'm moving on."

And she walked out.

~~~

NUPTIALS SANS GROOM

Andy crept down the hall, tip-toeing on stocking feet like a burglar. He stopped in front of the heavy oaken door and looked up and down the hall to make sure no one was around. He was safe. Stealthily, he leaned toward the door and pushed his ear against the cool dark wood. He thought he heard giggling. He hesitated. Opening the door could be dangerous.

Did he dare? He shook his head. It didn't matter what happened once he opened the door. Out here was much worse.

Steeling himself, he turned the brass knob, pulled the door open a crack, and slid inside.

And he was met with… screams.

"Andy!"

"Get out!"

"No, Andy! What the fuck!"

A charging wall of waving arms, jiggling boobs, round butts, long legs and angry faces forced him to push back into the door. There was nothing more terrifying than a wall of unbridled bridesmaids.

"What are you doing here, Andy?" a sultry voice said, cutting through the shrill cries. "The groom isn't allowed to see the bride before the wedding."

It was Lola, Emily's best friend, and the maid of honor. Lola stepped out of the wall of women and glared at him. She stood five feet eight inch tall, but in platform wedges she was basically a giant. The wedding was still two hours away, and Lola wasn't in bridesmaid mode yet. She was still in Lola mode, which meant that she was wearing a super tight black dress that plunged in the front showing off copious cleavage, hugged her middle showing off her fit form, and barely reached her thighs, threatening to reveal her legendary and highly extolled bottom.

"Andy, are you crazy? Get out of here. You can't see me yet," Emily said, her disembodied voice floating over the wall of bridesmaids.

"Why aren't you wearing any shoes?" Lola asked, looking down at his stocking feet suspiciously.

He shrugged. "I don't know," he admitted. "Look, you guys, it's crazy out there. You have no idea."

"That doesn't mean you should be in here," Lola said.

Lola was Emily's childhood friend. The two of them basically grew up together and they were closer than sisters. Her expression of indulgent disapproval looked very much like Emily's expression. Lola had a way of looking at him that made him think she was looking at him with Emily's eyes. It was disturbing, to say the least. He had no idea how two women who looked so different could have the same expressions.

Of course, there were some similarities between them. They were both tall—he had already accepted that Emily would be taller than him in the six-inch platforms she had chosen for the wedding—and they were both fit and curvaceous, but other than that they looked completely different. Emily was blonde with blue eyes and fair features, which gave the impression she was wholesome like an angel, while Lola was dark

84

and sultry, and had a dangerous air about her. They were so different but somehow so alike. They were like two sides of the same sexy coin. "Come on, Lola, please let me stay. I have to hide somewhere," he said, pressing his back into the door, as if he already knew that his decision to come into the room had been the wrong one.

"I don't think so, sweetheart. You know very well it's bad luck for the groom to see the bride in her dress before the wedding," Emily said from behind the bridesmaids.

"You're already dressed?" Andy asked, looking down at his t-shirt and stocking feet and growing even more nervous. Should he be dressed already? He had only his tuxedo pants on.

Lola snorted. Lola and Emily were always laughing at him.
"No, stupid," Emily giggled. "I'm just putting on my make-up."

"Then why can't I stay? I won't even look at the dress. I don't care for the dress anyway," Andy said.

There was a burst of indignation from the wall of bridesmaids, and Lola shook her head.

"Just because, Andy, that's why," she said, tapping her foot.

"Emily, come on, have a heart," Andy pleaded. "You don't know what it's like out there. Your dad is killing me."

Lola snorted. "And you call yourself a man! Phil's a pussycat," she said, shifting from one foot to the other in a way that made her tight dress ripple over her belly.

She was dangerous.

"He's a pussycat to you," Andy said, letting his eyes slide over Lola's body, "but he hates me." He wanted to say Emily's dad loved Lola because he wanted to fuck her—who didn't?—but he held his tongue. This was not the time to get on Lola's bad side.

"What do you expect? You are balling his daughter! Of course, he hates you," Lola said, and she swayed her hips.

Andy's jaw dropped, Lola shrugged, and Emily's snort of laughter burst from behind the wall of bridesmaids.

"Don't bust my balls, Lola," Andy whined. "Not today."

"Maybe they need busting," Lola said, biting her full lip.

Andy immediately felt his cock swelling. He gulped and looked at the ceiling. She was dangerous.

"Get out, Andy," Emily sighed in exasperation.

"Come on, Emily. Pretty please?" Andy whined.

There was a hum from the wall of bridesmaids. Lola turned, showing off an enticing flash of panty. The wall became a tight huddle. There were hisses and giggles. Then the huddle broke, and Emily pushed through the wall of bridesmaids.

"I tell you what. You can hide in here for ten minutes," she said. Her long hair was pinned up. She was wearing an ivory satin camisole, her perky nipples doing their best to poke through the shiny fabric, and silk ivory pantaloons that hugged her long legs. She looked good enough to eat.

"Are you sure, Emily?" Lola said. It was obvious she was speaking for the bridesmaids.

"It's fine, girls," Emily said. "Andy and I need to go over some plans for tonight."

Lola frowned, and there was a general grumbling from the group, followed by head nods. A consensus had been reached that he should be allowed to stay.

"It won't take long," Emily said with a smirk.

Andy didn't dare speak.

"You heard the lady, girls," Lola said. "Let's give the love birds ten."

The girls began to file out of the room, and Andy quickly stepped aside to get out of their way.

"Make it twenty, Lola," he said, as Lola swiveled by.

"If you think it'll take Emily twenty minutes to bust those balls, Andy, you should think again," she purred, running her tongue over her lips. Andy gulped, and his eyes chased her as she stepped out the door and lingered on her wiggling butt as she strutted away. Oh, she could walk with the best of them!

"Hello? Earth calling Andy," Emily said, making him jump.

"Um, yeah," he said as he spun around.

"I'm over here," she said, pointing to herself. "Or is there some other show you want to watch?"

He went to her. "No, babe," he said, holding out his hands. "I want to see you. Only you."

She grunted. "I'm sure you do."

He took her warm hands in his. "Why don't we get out of here and run to Las Vegas? No one would miss us."

She rolled her eyes. "Don't be stupid. Of course, they'll miss us," she said. "If we got out of here now right before the wedding, both my family and yours would kill you."

He slumped. "I know," he said. "But honestly, why do they have to make such a fuss?"

"Because, Andy, my sweet and lovely husband-to-be, it's really a big deal," Emily said. "They all know it. This is it. Our one chance. If this marriage thing doesn't work, well, you know what's going to happen to you, don't you?"

"Um, no," Andy stammered. "What's going to happen?"

"Let me put it to you this way. I'll spit you above a fire and eat you," Emily said with a giggle.

Andy looked into her eyes, and she looked into his, her gaze suddenly serious. In that moment he saw in her eyes something that made him shrink a little inwardly. He realized that Lola wasn't the only dangerous one. Then Emily laughed, and the spell of her gaze was broken. He leaned in to kiss her, but she turned her head away.

"Uh uh, you'll mess up my make-up," she said.

He sighed. "See what I mean? Why does it have to be so hard?"

She smiled and reached out to rub her hand over the front of his trousers.

"This is what's hard, sweetheart," she said, slowly rubbing his erection.

"You're just a little tense." She squeezed his cock. "You need to release that tension."

He let out a deep breath as she squeezed him.

"I'll take care of you. You'll be fine in no time," she said.

She undid his belt, then the button, then his fly. He reached for her.

"Uh uh," she said, waving her finger at him. "No touching. I'm not getting mussed and I'm not getting all sweaty. Not today. You'll have to wait till tonight to get the full treatment. This is just a little triage."

"But Emily," Andy whined, "it's been two weeks."

Two weeks of no sex, that had been Emily's pre-wedding prescription. To make their wedding night worth the wait, so she had said.

"Don't whine," she said, working his hard cock out of his boxer briefs.

"I know your big dick can't do without this tight little pussy of mine."

She tapped her crotch. "But the wait is almost over. In a few hours I'll be riding that cock like nobody's business. Till then you'll have to wait. Now come here." She gently tugged him by his cock, pulling him close.

"I just…" he started, but she raised her hand.

"Shh. Don't worry about a thing. I'll take good care of you," she cooed, and she slowly rubbed the head of his swollen cock over her satin camisole.

"Oh, that feels so good, Emily," he groaned, as his swollen head slid back and forth over the smooth material.

"I know how much you like it," she said. She folded the satin around his shaft and slid her hand up and down his length.

"Oh fuck," he moaned, as she stroked his throbbing cock with her satin camisole.

"That's my cock and don't you forget it," Emily cooed, stroking faster up and down his thick shaft.

She squeezed the head of his cock in the satin, and a shudder ran through him. She cupped his balls. His eyes fluttered. The sensations grew. She stopped.

"No, no, no, you bad boy," she whispered. "There will be no cumming on my wedding things."

"Please, don't stop, Emily," he groaned, as she pulled away.

90

"Who says I'm stopping?" she cooed. "I said I'd take care of you and take care of you I will. I want you to get up on that chair."

She pulled him toward a large table and pointed to the chair she had been sitting in when he came into the room. He started to sit down but she stopped him.

"No sitting," she said. "I'm not kneeling on this floor. Get up on it."

"OK," he grunted, stepping up on the chair.

"No, that's not going to work. Get up on the table." He did, his cock bobbing. "Perfect," she said, looking up at him.

His hard cock was nearly eye level and perfectly mouth level. She kissed the tip. He reached down and put both hands on her head. She pulled back.

"No touching the hair," she warned. "Let's just say, don't touch anything."

"Right," he said, pulling his hands back.

"Good boy," she said.

She looked up at him while she licked the underside of his cock.

"Oh, Emily," he moaned, relishing the feel of her tongue sliding up and down his hard shaft.

"I'll always take care of you, sweetheart," she cooed, taking his head in her mouth.

He shuddered while she slowly slid her plump lips down his shaft, taking him all the way down her throat till her nose was pressed into his belly.

"Oh god, Emily, you can suck dick," he moaned.

She slid off his cock and grinned up at him, a stream of spit connecting her lips to his head.

"That's why you love me," she said, licking her lips.

Holding his eyes with hers, she swirled her tongue around the tip of his cock. He shook and had to look away to keep from cumming.

"Can't take watching me fuck you with my mouth, Andy?" she giggled, taking his shaft in her hands and slowly stroking. "Will it make you cum too soon if you watch your cock slide in my mouth like you're fucking my tight pussy?"

"I can take it," he moaned, but he didn't look down as she took him in her mouth.

He looked at anything but her. The dressing room had large casement windows on the far wall, but their bottom halves were curtained for privacy. Standing on the table, he could see out the top half. He could see the sidewalk and the sitting area right outside the windows where the bridesmaids had gathered. Lola was there, too, ten feet away drinking from a bottle of water.

Emily swallowed his cock and slid off, slowly fucking him with her mouth. Those lips on his cock felt so good. She licked his head. Andy looked out at Lola. Lola sipped her water. She had a sexy mouth. Then she glanced up at him. Their eyes met.

"Fuck," Andy groaned, as Emily swallowed his cock.

Outside the window, Lola grinned, as if she knew what was going on. Her back was to the other girls so they couldn't see when she slid the bottle of water over her lips just as Emily slid his cock over her lips.

"Oh fuck," Andy groaned.

Slowly, Lola slid the bottle into her mouth, her luscious lips slipping down the long neck.

"Fuck, fuck, fuck," Andy groaned, as Emily slid her lips down his thick shaft.

Emily started fucking him faster, using her mouth and hand in unison, twisting her hand and her lips up and down his shaft. The feeling was incredible. Just outside the window, Lola started sucking the bottle, sliding it in and out from between her lips. Between what he was feeling and what he was seeing, it was too much for him. His body trembled.

"I'm cumming," he groaned.

"Cum for me, Andy," Emily cooed, looking up at him while stroking him.

His orgasm came like an explosion. A single hot spurt of cum escaped Emily's lips, shooting on her cheek and over her eye into her eyebrow, before she clamped her lips over his head, sucking as his cock throbbed. He shot gush after gush into her eager mouth and she swallowed it all to the last drop, slowly stroking him to get every bit. Outside, Lola was licking her lips, slowly working her tongue. Her eyes were sparkling with fiendish delight.

"Feeling better?" Emily asked, slowly stroking his cock.

He met her eyes just as she used her finger to scoop up the cum that got away. When she licked the cum clean, his legs felt weak and his cock throbbed, growing hard again.

"You'll have to wait for tonight to get more," she said, stepping away. "Now go and get ready. We're getting married."

**

The wedding ceremony went without a hitch. The church was beautiful. Emily was beautiful behind her veil. Lola was dangerous as always.

When she slowly parted her lips, the minister stammered over the vows, and he practically moaned, "I do", when she ran the tip of her tongue over her lips. But he recovered, and no one seemed to notice his raging erection. At least, no one mentioned it.

After the religious ceremony, the wedding moved to a hotel downtown, and the party started. Emily and the bridesmaids changed into their party dresses. Emily still wore white but the dress was a low-cut body-con dress that hugged her curves. The bridesmaids wore black. At the dinner, with the champagne flowing, Emily stroked his cock under the table as her father gave a speech about giving his daughter away.

Thirty minutes later, after the dinner had moved to the hall, Emily's stalwart father was giving a different speech to Lola. A speech that involved comments on how great she was looking, how she had grown up into a fine woman, and how he could still remember her running around the house naked. It was very sweet. How he was drooling into her cleavage wasn't quite as sweet.

"Having fun, husband of mine?" Emily asked as they tripped the light fantastic around the dance floor.

"Great time, wife of mine," he said, slowly spinning her. "But I'm ready to go upstairs."

"Are you already tired, husband?" she giggled.

"Tired of all these people, wife," he said.

"Ahh. Do you want to be alone, husband?" She laughed, sliding close to him.

"Yes, wife," he said.

"Oh," she cooed. Then she brushed her lips against his ear. "Do you want to get me alone to ravage me?"

Her voice tickled his ear. He grabbed her ass and pulled her to him. She opened her legs and slid up his thigh so that his hardness pressed between her legs.

"Yes, wife," he whispered, kissing her neck. "I want to get you alone to fuck you."

"That's good, husband," she moaned as he rained kisses down her neck, "because I need a good fucking. You'd better be ready to fuck me like you mean it."

"I'll fuck you, Emily," he growled.

She ground down on his cock, slowly rocking her hips back and forth, back and forth. "I need your dick, Andy. I need it deep inside me, filling me, stretching me."

She bit his earlobe. He shuddered.

"I'm going to ride you like you're my favorite horsey," she breathed, sucking his earlobe and rocking her hips. "I'm going to fuck you silly and suck you dry."

He stopped dancing and looked at her. She bit her lip and rocked against his cock.

"Then what are we still doing here, Emily?" he groaned. "Let's go. Now!"

She laughed. "I'm going to tell my dad we're going."

He groaned. "Not your dad, come on. You're going to tell him what we're going to do?"

"No, stupid," she giggled. "Everyone already knows what we're going to do."

"Right," he sighed.

She laughed. "Why don't you see if you can find Lola?"

"OK," he muttered.

"I think she might be outside with Cole."

Andy raised his eyebrows. "With Cole?"

"Yeah. What's wrong with Cole?" Emily asked.

"Nothing," he said, "if you like the biker slash psycho kind of guy."
"Lola's always liked bad boys."

"You guys are best friends, so how did I end up with you?" he asked.
"You may be a good guy," Emily giggled, "but you've got a bad boy's
dick." And she reached down and squeezed his cock. "Now stop wast-
ing time."

"Meet you at the elevator in ten," he said.

"I'll be sucking your cock on the elevator in eleven," she said with a
meaningful grin.

**

There was a hallway off the banquet room. That was how they had tum-
bled into the reception after the wedding. It was also how the smokers
got outside when they went to have a smoke. That was where Andy
went. There was a hop in his step as he bustled down the hall. He was
anxious to get to the elevator, to get upstairs, to get inside Emily.

The fire exit at the end of the hall was propped open with a chair. He
slid past the door into the alleyway and darkness. He was thinking
about Emily and her mouth. Would she dare suck his dick on the ele-

vator? He knew she would. Emily looked like an angel but she fucked like a devil. He was imagining her on her knees, her lips locked on his shaft, when he heard Lola. He was about to call her name but her words stopped him cold.

"Come on, Cole, don't you want to fuck me?" she said in her husky, sexy voice.

Andy stopped.

Lola and Cole were in the alley next to a huge potted hibiscus, no more than fifteen feet away from him. The alley was a dead end with only the fire door to the hall and the backdoor to a boutique. The boutique was closed at this time of night and the alley was deserted. It was dark, but there were tiny lights that looked like Christmas lights strung overhead.

Their soft light made the alley look almost festive and allowed Andy to see what Lola and Cole were doing while he remained cast in shadow. Lola had her back against the concrete wall. Her arms were stretched out, resting on Cole's shoulders and she was swaying her body in a way that made Andy's already hard cock ache. Cole's hands were on her waist. He said something, but Andy didn't hear what.

"Yes, I'm sure, Cole. I want you to fuck me right here and right now," she cooed, and she ran a hand down his chest.

Frozen in place, Andy watched. His heart was pounding and his cock was throbbing.

Cole put his hand on Lola's cheek. She turned her face into his palm. Cole ran his thumb over her lower lip. Lola reacted to his touch by arching her back and rolling her hips like a cat being rubbed. He ran his thumb slowly back and forth while she twisted her body. She cupped one of her breasts and squeezed, and her other hand slowly ran up her leg, pulling her short black dress up and up and up.

"You want to fuck?" Cole growled.

"Yes," Lola moaned, and she took his thumb in her mouth, slowly sliding her lips down its length.

Andy swallowed, and he frantically rubbed his throbbing cock through his trousers. He couldn't believe what he was seeing.

Cole leaned into Lola. They kissed. The kiss was long and hot. Cole pressed his body into hers, pinning Lola to the concrete wall. Lola spread her long legs, lifting one and wrapping it around Cole's waist. Cole slid a hand under her round ass and pulled her close. Lola twisted and rolled her body into his as he pressed her against the wall. They kissed. She put her right hand on his back, pulling him harder against her. He held her left arm by the wrist, pinning her arm over her head. Their kiss lingered as they rubbed against each other.

Andy was transfixed. He squeezed his cock, not daring to move, not able to look away.

Their rubbing became frantic. Cole dropped Lola's wrist and put both hands on her ass while she wrapped both legs around his middle. They broke their kiss, and Cole buried his head in Lola's neck. Lola's head turned. Her eyes were closed. Their bodies rocked together, faster and faster. Cole's breaths came out in rasps. Lola was moaning, her mouth an orgasmic O. Her eyes fluttered, then opened.

And she looked right at Andy.

The world stopped as their eyes met. Andy knew she'd say something. She'd stop and point at him. Accuse him. He'd be caught and Emily would find out. His wedding night would go from the best night of his life to the worst.

Lola smiled, and then the smile became a snarl. She began moving more frantically, almost desperately, her firm thighs flexing as she pulled Cole to her with her strong legs, grinding against him. She never broke eye contact with Andy. She never looked away.

Relief and desire flooded Andy, making his cock even harder.

Lola and Cole humped against the wall until Lola pulled Cole's head back with a handful of his dark hair. "I need that dick," she snarled. Her eyes were slanted toward Andy.

Cole didn't answer, but he stepped back. Lola kissed him, then she slowly lowered herself to her knees. Andy watched, mesmerized. She worked Cole's belt buckle, then his button, then his fly, and in a second his hard pink cock was in her face.

"Hmm," she cooed as she kissed the tip, but she kept her eyes on Andy. It was too much for Andy. He didn't care about getting caught. He didn't care about anything. Frantically, he fumbled with his belt, his button, his fly, and pulled out his cock.

"Mmm, very nice," Lola moaned, and there was the slightest widening of her dark eyes as her hungry gaze fell on Andy's swollen member. Cole's cock was nicely sized but Andy's was bigger and thicker, and she saw that.

"It's so big and thick," Lola moaned, taking Cole in her mouth but staring at Andy's dick.

Andy stroked himself as she sucked, moving his hand up and down his shaft as her luscious lips slid up and down Cole's cock. Cole put a hand on the back of Lola's head and pushed her down. She took all of him. She never took her eyes off Andy as he stroked his length. Cole pulled back and thrust his cock in Lola's mouth, faster and faster, fucking her mouth. Watching them, Andy stroked faster. Still sucking Cole's cock, Lola slipped a hand under her dress and pulled it over her hips. Then she slid her fingers between her legs and started rubbing her pussy. Then it was all rubbing and sucking and stroking.

Suddenly, Lola pulled back. "I need that dick in my pussy," she slurped, her sensuous eyes on Andy's cock.

She stood up, and Cole pushed her back into the wall. She pulled her dress up around her middle, lifter her legs, and pulled Cole to her by his cock.

"Fuck me," she moaned, wrapping her legs around Cole and staring into Andy's eyes.

Andy wouldn't have had to be asked twice, and Cole was no different. He surged toward Lola, and she let out a hiss and arched her back when he slid his cock inside her waiting pussy.

"Fuck me," she groaned, twisting and writhing to give his hard cock access to her wetness.

Cole thrust his hips and Lola cried out, wrapping her arms around him. They stayed like that for a moment, their breathing coming in short, sharp gasps. Then Cole started fucking her.

"Oh, I need that big dick inside me," Lola moaned, her eyes on Andy. She rocked and rolled as Cole thrust and Andy stoked.

"Fuck, fuck, fuck," Lola groaned, and the two of them started moving faster.

Andy stroked faster, too, Lola's moans driving his sensations higher and higher. He was going to cum.

"I'm cumming," Lola moaned.

And Andy felt his explosion surge through him just as someone tapped him on the shoulder.

**

"What did you think you were doing, Andy?" Emily barked.

They were in the bridal suite. Andy was sitting on the loveseat like a forlorn schoolboy caught cheating on a final exam, while Emily paced. She'd walk to the bed, turn and walk back to him, then spin away as if she couldn't stand to look at him.

"Anyone could have walked in and caught you with your dick in your hand," she ranted, turning halfway to the bed and shaking her veil at him. "What if it had been my father who caught you beating off?"

The word 'father' made Andy noticeably shrink.

"What were you thinking?" she cried, throwing her arms in the air in

102

exasperation.

Andy didn't answer. She shook her head and resumed her pacing. His ecstasy in the alley had been short lived, cut off when he had spun around and seen his new wife staring at him. Startled and in mid-climax, he had shot cum on her dress, rope after streaming rope, and Emily had just watched the spurting cum splatter on her. Then she'd shaken her head in disgust and stalked away. Andy had chased her, fumbling to get his cock in his pants, while back in the alley Lola was still moaning, her ecstatic "Yes, yes, yes…" chasing him down the hall. Emily had stalked through the few remaining stragglers from the reception with Andy trailing a step behind her.

"They're in a hurry," someone had said as they went by.

Andy had nodded and gave a half-hearted smile. Emily hadn't said anything, but her hands had been balled into fists. They had ridden in the elevator in silence. There hadn't been any dick sucking on the way up. Then they had entered the bridal suite where Emily had begun his systematic evisceration.

"What do you have to say for yourself, Andy?" Emily barked.

Andy jumped and tried to say something, anything, but he couldn't seem to be able to string words together.

"You were beating off in an alley, Andy. You must have something to say about that," Emily said.

"Lola was fucking Cole in an alley," Andy said meekly.

Emily rolled her eyes, and Andy knew he said the wrong thing.

"And you were watching them fuck and jerking off," Emily growled. "This isn't about what Lola was doing." She shook her head. "Fuck! You were supposed to find her, not masturbate over her."

She spun away, took three steps, and spun back.

"You were beating off watching my best friend," she cried. "In an alley! Your cock out for the world to see!"

She waited.

Andy's head hung low between his shoulders.

She waited.

"Um, I'm sorry," Andy tried.

"Sorry?" she huffed. "I bet you're sorry. It's our wedding night."

"I'm really, really sorry," Andy tried again.

Emily shook her head and let out a long breath.

"You'd better be glad you've already got your rocks off because you're not cumming inside my pussy anytime soon, buster," she said, and she tapped her hand just below her belly. "This little kitty is an Andy No-Go Zone for the foreseeable future."

"Come on, Emily," Andy whined. "I'm sorry. I know it was a foolish thing to do, but we haven't had sex for two weeks because you wanted to wait till the wedding, and then what you said about what you were going to do to me in the elevator just had me so turned on, and…" He paused, and hesitated.

She scowled but she didn't say anything.

"When I saw them fucking, it was too much," he said, and quickly looked down.

"Let me see if I have this straight. You were just horny because you've had no sex for two weeks and you were thinking about my lips wrapped around your big cock," Emily said.

Andy nodded vigorously.

"And when you were stroking your cock watching Cole fuck Lola against the wall, when his cock was pounding her pussy..." She moved her hips like she was thrusting. "...You were just thinking about your hard dick sliding in my mouth." And she slid her finger in her mouth and out, her lips lingering on her finger. "That's why you were beating off in the alley?"

"That's right," Andy gulped, his cock rock hard again as he watched Emily slide her finger over her plump lips.

She snorted. "Come on, Andy, do you think I'm blind? I saw you staring at Lola's jiggling ass earlier. You weren't thinking about me. You were thinking about my best friend's tight pussy wrapped around your cock."

"No way. I was just looking, Emily," Andy cried. "It was nothing, just looking. You look at guys. I've seen you look at Cole."

"Yes, Andy, I've looked at Cole. He's hot, but I don't beat off in an alley looking at him," she snarled. "There's a big difference."

She stared at him. He stared at the ground. She sighed.

"Well, I'm glad you like to watch fucking because that's all you'll be doing for the near future," she said, and she turned and walked away from him.

"What does that mean?" Andy asked cautiously.

Emily didn't answer. She went to the dressing table and unzipped her big cosmetics bag. She began digging furiously through it, dumping make-up all over the place.

"Oh, I'm so glad I didn't leave this one behind," she said, pulling something large out of the bag.

She spun around and thrust out a huge dildo toward him. Andy gaped at the thick phallus.

"You brought a dildo on our wedding night?" Andy asked, incredulous. Emily scowled. "I had an inkling you'd let me down tonight, but I thought you'd get yourself too drunk to fuck me properly. I had no idea I'd catch you hand-fucking yourself while you were perving over my best friend."

She marched toward him, thrusting the dildo in his face. The dildo was bright pink with big balls and a suction cup. She kissed the tip lovingly. "Edward is always reliable," she said, looking at the dildo with deep affection. "He never ever lets me down."

"Edward?" Andy said, staring at the huge pink dong. "You named your dildo?"

"Of course, I named him. Edward has been with me a long time for a lot of fucking."

Andy watched as she rubbed the dildo down her belly over the stains of his cum.

"Edward… You didn't name it after Edward Cullen, did you?" he asked.

"After the vampire from Twilight?"

"I did," Emily said superciliously. "And Edward is going to give me a very fulfilling wedding night, fulfilling and filling. It's going to be very filling with Edward inside me." And she ran the tip of her tongue around the tip of the huge dildo.

Andy squirmed, his eyes locked on the tip of her tongue as it traced the head of the dildo. "Come on, Emily, don't torture me," he whined, squirming against his erection.

"You're going to watch me and Edward fuck, Andy," Emily said. "And you're not going to touch your cock while you watch."

Andy stared at her, not sure he was hearing right.

"Do you understand me, Andy?" she snarled.

"Emily, but that's crazy," he whined.

"Oh, you think so?" she said. "Do want to stay married or not?"

"Yes, I do," Andy cried. "With all my heart I do, but..."

"No buts," she said. "You'll do what I say or this is our last night together. It's really that simple." And she shook the dildo at him.

There was a long silence. Andy squirmed under her stare.

"Ok, I'll watch," Andy finally said.
"Without touching yourself."

"Yes."

"Great," she said brightly. "Now. I had something really special planned for us tonight, but since you ruined it, it looks like it has to be just for me and Edward."

"It doesn't have to be, Emily," Andy said.

"Shut up," she snarled, "and get undressed."

He got up and stripped while she watched without saying a word. She looked down at his erection and rolled her eyes.

"You're still hard," she said. "After everything that happened. Doesn't that cock know any better?"

"I'm hard for you, Emily," he said. "All for you."

She snorted. "You're hard for pussy."

He started to protest but she interrupted him.

"You will sit there and watch," she said.

He sat, his cock pointing toward the ceiling in expectation.

"Ok, this is what I was planning when I said we should wait for two weeks," she said, and she went over to one of the bedside tables and fiddled with her phone.

Music started playing. It was slow and sensuous with a beat, boom, boom, boom, like Andy's heart. She tossed the dildo on the bed, turned toward Andy, and started to move to the music.

"I thought about this night for a long time, Andy," she said, rolling her hips slowly from side to side. "I wanted it to be special."

"I'm sorry," Andy said, watching her move. She was so sexy that his cock was getting even harder.

"Don't talk, Andy," she said, as she slowly pulled her dress off one shoulder, then the other.

Moving to the beat of the music, she shimmied out of the tight dress, slowly pushing it down over her full breasts—she hadn't worn a bra and her perfect breasts sprang out at him—down her flat belly—her muscles rippling beneath her skin—over one round hip, twist, over the other hip, and finally the dress fell to the floor. She stood there wearing only a white thong and high heels, slowly rocking her hips.

It had been two weeks since he saw her naked, and she had spent that time making her perfect body even more perfect. She had never looked better. Looking at her made Andy ache.

"This was going to be for you, Andy," she said, and she slid the thong over her legs and let it fall on the ground.

"Emily," he breathed.

Her frown shut him up.

She turned, swinging her hips, and walked to the cosmetics bag. She pulled out a bottle of oil. She walked back in front of him, standing just out of reach. Looking down at him, fierce, she tipped up the bottle and golden oil dripped down on her skin, drops raining on her breasts, her belly, her thighs.

"You should be doing this, Andy," she said, slowly rubbing the oil across her body.

She worked the oil over her skin. She dripped more oil on her belly, then she threw the bottle away. Using both hands, she worked the oil over her belly, then she rubbed it down her stomach, over her mons, and between her legs.

"Ohh," she sighed, rubbing herself slowly.

"Oh, Emily," Andy gasped, as her fingers slid over her folds.

She kept rubbing her pussy. With her other hand, she squeezed a hard nipple between her fingers.

"Ohh," she moaned, arching her back.

Andy gasped.

With one hand, Emily cupped her pussy, while her other hand glided across her body to her ass. She pressed both hands between her legs, her hips rocking, and she slid one finger in her pussy and another in her ass.

"Oh yes," she moaned as she was fingering herself.

"Oh dear god, Emily," Andy gasped.
"Fuck," Emily suddenly exclaimed. "I need more." And she stared at him.

Andy's cock swelled.

As if she could read his mind, she shook her head. "I'm not talking about you, sparky," she snarled. "It's Edward time." And she reached for the big dildo. "Time to relocate! Come on, Andy."

**

From his place on the toilet, Andy watched Emily stick Edward to the glass wall of the shower stall. The water was streaming, but the stall was so large she was out of the water.

"Does this look about right?" she asked him, reaching down to stroke the dildo.

"Right for what?" Andy asked.

"Does it look like Edward's the right height?" she asked, looking down at the dildo.

Andy shrugged. She frowned, then got down on her hands and knees.

Her ass was in the falling water and the dildo hung right in front of her face.

"Edward," she moaned, sliding her lips over the dildo.

She slid her lips down the shaft of the dildo, moving slowly up and down its length while wiggling her body. The water falling on her beaded up and rolled across her smooth oiled skin. Her perky breasts hung down, her hard nipples pointing slightly out. She slid one hand down her belly and between her legs. She sucked Edward.

"Fuck," Andy moaned, as he watched her deep-throat the pink dildo. Emily sucked as she fingered herself. Her hand moved fast. Andy's hand shifted to his cock. She stopped sucking Edward and glared at him.

"Don't you dare touch yourself," she moaned, still fingering herself.

Andy dropped his hand to his side. His cock was aching. She nodded, and put her lips back around Edward and sucked. She sucked and wiggled until Andy thought he might die, then she stopped.

"I'm so wet," she moaned. "I think my little pussy is ready for Edward now. What do you think, Andy? Are you ready to see Edward spread my pussy wide? Are you ready to see me fuck Edward like Cole fucked Lola?"

Andy could only groan.

"You'd better be ready," she said.

Emily crawled around and pushed her butt toward the dildo. "Oh, I know I'm ready. I need you, Edward," she moaned, pushing her ass up and rubbing her wet pussy over the dildo back and forth, back and forth.

Andy could see every inch of the pink silicone dick as it slid between his wife's legs. It was torture seeing her body writhe, but he couldn't stop watching.

"Fuck me, Edward," she moaned. She reached back between her legs, took hold of the fat dildo, and slowly pushed the head to her wet opening.

Andy stopped breathing when she arched her back and rocked her ass back, letting the dildo slowly slide inside her. As the dildo slid deeper and deeper inside her, she made keening noises that were pure pleasure.

"Oh, Edward, you're so fucking deep in my pussy," she moaned, her ass cheeks flattened against the glass wall.

Then she slowly rolled her hips, grinding her ass against the glass.

"Fuck, Emily, you're killing me like this," Andy whispered.

She looked back at him, grinning.

"This would have been you, Andy," she said, sliding off the dildo, then slowly siding it back inside her pussy. "You would have fucked me like this."

Her grin became a look of pure ecstasy as she impaled herself on the thick dildo.

"Harder, Edward, harder, harder, "she moaned.

She moved faster and faster, her ass slapping into the glass. Andy could only watch as she rode the dildo, her rolling body moving with abandon. Seeing her ride that silicone dick made his cock ache.

"Oh, you're going to make me cum, Edward," she cried, and her body shook.

She shifted back so her ass was flattened against the glass, and she gyrated on the dildo. Her body was quivering, as if the dildo was sending electrical charges bursting through her pussy.

"What do you think, Andy?" she moaned. "Do you like watching Edward fuck me? Was it worth being a perv? Is this better than watching my best friend get fu….?"

Her last word become intelligible as her legs began to quiver. She closed her eyes and threw back her head.

"Oh, I'm cumming, I'm cumming," she groaned, as she slammed her ass into the glass wall driving the dildo even deeper in her wet pussy.

The spectacle was too much for Andy. Without ever touching his cock, he exploded, sending gouts of cum onto his chest and belly.

**

Spent, Emily lay on the big bed in the dark room. Andy was on the ground.

"What can I do to make it better?" he asked.

There was a long stretch of silence, and he thought she might be asleep.

"Lingerie," she said sleepily.

"What?"

"You heard me," she said. "After you've had enough punishment, you're going to buy me a boatload of lingerie, sweetheart."

**

Andy stood on the sidewalk in front of the steps that led to a fancy storefront: black cast iron façade, ornate windows, an antique door with a brass knocker. It looked like an old Parisian boutique that you only see on postcards. Above the door there was a sign that said: Rendezvous. He looked down at the sheet of paper in his hand on which there were written his instructions:

Go to Rendezvous (there was an address) and ask for Ms. McKay. Do whatever she tells you. No exceptions. Emily.

He hesitated. He looked up at the door. Two leggy women walked past him, smiling at him as they pranced up the steps. He saw the flash of something colorful under one of their skirts. When they opened the door, the high, happy tinkle of a bell spilled into the street. They disappeared inside the store, and Andy was left alone staring.

He had heard about Rendezvous before. Emily and Lola had both worked there when they were in college, and they still shopped there, but that was all he knew about it. He felt silly going into a lingerie store all by himself, but if he ever wanted to replace Edward between his wife's legs, he had no choice but to go inside and shop like a demon.

With a sigh of resignation, he trudged up the steps and pushed open the door. A bell tinkled over his head. He looked up and when he looked back down, as if conjured by magic, a beautiful woman stood before him.

"You can leave your shoes over there," she said, pointing to a shoe rack by the door.

"Um, ok," Andy said.

He did his best not to look at her, but it was an effort not to gape. She was wearing a black tulle bodysuit with flower embroidery in strategic places that had the effect of making her look even more naked than she actually was. She was irresistible, but he had to remind himself that he was already in the doghouse for looking and he wasn't about to repeat that mistake. Especially when he was doing his damndest to make up for it. But venturing into the strange world of lingerie and trying to avoid temptations was turning out to be as difficult as Hercules's trials. The woman was so gorgeous and so... well... basically naked, and he was hard, so, so hard. It was impossible not to look.

"I have an appointment with Ms. McKay," Andy said, squirming. "My wife used to work here. Emily. Emily Swallow," he added, as if invoking her name would inoculate him from the dangers he was facing.

The woman smiled and bounced on her toes making her full breasts jiggle. Andy quickly looked at his feet.

"So you're Emily's guy," she said.

Andy thought he heard something in her voice that said she knew all about him. Had Emily told everyone why he was there? What he had done?

He nodded. "That's me," he said, his eyes wandering over her succulent curves, her belly button, the shadow of her nipples, the curve of her neck, and….

Oh, his treacherous eyes and her tempting body. He was dying.

He shifted uncomfortably, his hardness straining against his pants. After one week of watching Emily fuck Edward the Dildo and not being allowed to even touch himself he was ready to explode. This beautiful woman was torture.

"I'm Tori," she said, wiggling delectably. "Ms. McKay is waiting for you. Follow me, I'll take you to her."

She spun on her heel sending her hair flying and started walking. Andy chased after her, trying not to look at her bouncing ass. But when he looked away, he saw another delectable woman in even more revealing lingerie, and then another, and another. There were sexy women everywhere. There was nowhere safe for him to look but up. He admired the copper bowed wreath ceiling tiles. He looked at the chrome-finished crystal chandeliers. He looked at the red wallpaper and the stacks of lingerie that were displayed on tables everywhere.

"What do you have there, Tori?" a tall, dark woman with ample curves asked. She cast a dark-eyed look in Andy's direction.

"This is Emily's guy," Tori said, still walking.

"Ahh, that guy," the tall, dark woman said, taking a closer look at him. "Emily has good taste. He's delicious."

"No snacking on the clock, Robin," Tori said.

Andy felt himself blushing. What was Emily thinking sending him here? There was no way he'd make it out of this man-pit alive. He was contemplating an escape when Tori stopped.

"Ms. McKay, your appointment is here," she said.

A group of women turned. They were all gathered around a tall, slim… man. The man was looking at himself in a long mirror. He was wearing a pair of bright blue satin panties without any sense of self-conscious-ness. He must have felt Andy's eyes on him because he looked up. Their eyes met and he smiled, then he went back to admiring himself in the mirror.

"Andy," a tall, attractive woman dressed in a black satin camisole and black satin panties said, "I'm Ms. McKay. Emily told me you'd be com-ing by today."

"Um, yes," Andy said. He couldn't help feeling a little at a disadvantage. What exactly had Emily told this woman?

"I know everything," Ms. McKay said, as if reading his thoughts. "That is why I'm going to do my best to get you back into Emily's…" She paused, then her lips quirked into a smile. "…Good graces, shall we say?"

"Do you think you can do that?" Andy said.

"I've known Emily a long time," she said, "and if anything will bring her around, it's silk and satin."

"But I don't know anything about lingerie," Andy said.

"That is why you are here, to learn," Ms. McKay said. "I've planned something very special for you."

She smiled at him. Her smile was warm, reassuring, but at the same time it was a little terrifying. Andy had never met anyone so self-assured. It was remarkably attractive. He couldn't not look at her.

"It's just that… Well, if Emily told you what happened…" he started, but didn't know how to go on.

"Rendezvous is a special place, Andy," Ms. McKay said. "You might have noticed that already. It's a safe place where people are free to be who they are. This is a place to be sexy and to see and admire what's sexy. There's nothing wrong with looking around here."

He nodded. Emily knew exactly what she was doing when she sent him here.

"Good," Ms. McKay said. "Come with me."

Andy accompanied Ms. McKay and, following her dictate that it was all right to look, kept his eyes on her round bottom as she strode through the boutique.

"Does everyone working here wear lingerie?" Andy asked, as he walked past the fourth woman clad in nothing but panties, a push-up bra, and thigh highs.

"We all love lingerie, so that's what we wear," Ms. McKay said.

"Was it like this when Emily and Lola worked here?" he asked.

"It certainly was," Ms. McKay said.

Andy could see Lola parading around in lingerie—he had seen her often enough since he had been dating Emily—but Emily… He couldn't see it.

"Emily was one of our most popular girls," Ms. McKay said. "She and Lola were quite a team."

"I would have liked to see that, "Andy said.

That would have been a deadly duo.

Across the store, Andy saw Robin. She was with a man in a suit. She was wearing a purple bustier and purple thong, with garter, thigh-highs, and heels. She was slowly spinning in front of the man, while he ran his eyes all over her with undisguised appreciation.

Had Emily practiced this kind of customer service?

"Emily was one of our best finishers," Ms. McKay said. "We sent her in when we had difficult customers. She always made the sale and they all left smiling."

"Oh," Andy said.

Imagining Emily with the man instead of Robin, he felt a stab of jealousy. Jealousy that was mixed with an eruption of desire.

They walked toward the back of the boutique and through a short hall.

The walls were opaque and Andy saw silhouettes, naked silhouettes.

It was a heartbeat before he realized that they were walking past the dressing rooms and that behind the opaque walls there were people changing. Two sensual silhouettes in one of the dressing rooms caught his eye. They were tall and leggy. For some reason they made him think of Emily and Lola. They weren't trying anything on. These silhouettes were locked together, sliding up and down each other's bodies. He stopped breathing as he watched silhouette hands slide over silhouette bottoms.

What kind of place was this?

"This way, Andy," Ms. McKay's voice broke into his reverie.

He didn't realize he had stopped walking and was staring at the tangled silhouettes. Her voice got him moving. She led him through an arched doorway blocked by a sheer curtain. She pulled the curtain to the side and they stepped into a large room.

"This is our showroom," Ms. McKay said, leading him down a runway.

At the end of the runway, down a step, was a two-person leather chaise. "Sit down, please," Ms. McKay said.

Andy slumped into the plush chaise, not certain what to expect. Ms. McKay slid next to him. Dangerously close, he thought. He could feel the body heat coming off of her. Without any prompting that he could see, music started playing. It was low, jazzy, but with a beat.

"After talking to Emily I prepared a very special exhibition for you," Ms. McKay said, patting his thigh.

Andy jumped.

"Relax, Andy. Emily gave me a free hand," Ms. McKay said, squeezing his leg. "And I assured her that I'd take care of you personally."

She rubbed her hand up his leg.

"Really?" Andy said, his voice breaking as her hand was getting very close to his aching erection.

"Really," Ms. McKay said, her hand gliding over his pants and sliding over his bulge. "Trust me." And she squeezed.

Andy let out something between a moan and a cry.

"Now watch," she said, motioning with her head toward the runway.

As if cued, a beautiful tall woman wearing a pink corset, matching pink satin panties and pink thigh-highs burst through the curtain and paraded before him. The beautiful tall woman in the pink corset was followed by another beautiful woman, this one petite and round and wearing a sheer red babydoll.

"I thought it would be a good idea to give an overview of the kind of lingerie Rendezvous carries," Ms. McKay said. "It will help you decide what you might want to surprise Emily with."

She punctuated her words by rubbing his hard cock. She rubbed up and down his length as the beautiful petite woman did a spin right in front of him, her juicy body moving in wonderful ways.

"Do you like babydolls?" Ms. McKay asked, still rubbing his cock.

"Yes," Andy breathed.

The woman in the babydoll strode away and another woman strutted into the room. She was wearing a black lace lingerie set with matching thigh-highs

"Lace is beautiful and always looks good on, but lingerie isn't only about how it looks," Ms. McKay said. "Lingerie is also about how it feels under your touch." When she said 'feels', she squeezed his cock.

He groaned.

"That sounds great," he stammered, his eyes locked on the woman on the runway who was leaning toward him giving him a view of her cleavage.

"The feel of lingerie is something that's often overlooked when people shop for lingerie, "Ms. McKay said. She took his hand and pulled it to her breast. "Feel," she said.

Andy let her slide his hand over breast, her diamond hard nipple pressing into his palm.

"The feel is just as important as the look," she said, rubbing his cock. "How does that feel?"

"So good," Andy moaned, squeezing her full breast.

Another woman burst through the curtain wearing a bright blue satin camisole, matching satin panties, and white thigh-highs.

"Do you see anything you like?" Ms. McKay asked, slowly rubbing his cock.

"Yes…" he stammered, watching the woman in blue satin and squeezing Ms. McKay's breast.

"Has Emily showed off any satin for you?" Ms. McKay asked.

"She has," Andy gulped.

Their first date had ended up in Emily's bed, but she had said she didn't fuck on the first date. Instead she had straddled him like a good little cowgirl.

"No touching," she had said.

She had been wearing a tiny tank top that was cropped just across her nipples, so her boobs hung out, and black satin panties. He had been naked, and she had rubbed her satin-covered pussy over his cock, back and forth, over and over, pressing his hardness down on his belly.

Finally, she had spun around and had made him cum by sliding the smooth satin over his dick. That had been the first time he got the satin treatment, and it hadn't been the last. Lately it was Edward the Dildo that was getting to rub over satin.

"Did you like it?" Ms. McKay asked.

"Yeah. It was amazing," Andy groaned.

She rubbed his cock faster while he leaned back.

"Rubbing can feel so good," she said, slipping his hand down her black satin camisole toward her panties.

"So good," Andy breathed, thrusting forward so his cock pressed into her hand. He relished the feel of the slick satin under his fingers as she pressed his hand against her warm mound.

"You need to really feel," she said, squeezing his cock. "Get your cock out."

Andy didn't hesitate. He fumbled with his belt and fly, and quickly pulled out his hard cock. Ms. McKay looked at his massive erection and smiled. She reached under her slip and pulled down her panties, pulling the black satin gracefully over her knees and stepping out of them. Then she reclined next to him and she reached out with the hand holding the black satin, closing it around his thick shaft. She held him for a quivering instant, while his body was trembling from the sensation, then she began to slowly stroke him.

"It feels good, doesn't it, Andy?" she whispered in his ear.

"Oh yes," he moaned as she slowly stroked.

"Good. Now get ready for something really special," Ms. McKay said.

"Special?" he moaned. What could be more special than this?

"Oh, yes," she said, and she kissed his cheek.

Her lips were soft and warm. He desperately wanted to feel them slip around the head of his cock, but she got up.

"Wait," he gasped.

She gave his cock one last squeeze. "Don't worry," she said. "The show's not over yet." And she strutted down the runway, giving him a smile as she went through the curtain.

Andy sat there, waiting, his anxious, hard cock pointing toward the ceiling. The wait wasn't long but it felt like forever. Then two women appeared through the curtain. They were both tall, slim, and curvy. One of them was fair and was wearing a white tank and white satin panties. The other was dark and was wearing a black tank and black satin panties.

Andy gulped.

The one in black was Lola.

The one in white was Emily.

**

"Emily," Andy gasped, looking up at his wife and then at her best friend.

Emily smiled. "It looks like you're having fun," she said, her sparkling eyes falling on his hard cock.

Andy grabbed his dick. "Emily," he stammered. "It's not what it looks like…"

Lola snorted. She was looking down at his cock, too. "It looks like you've been caught with your big cock in your hand again, Andy." Andy grimaced. Emily laughed.

"It's quite alright, Andy. Relax," she said. "Ms. McKay must have told you that this is a safe place."

Andy nodded.

"Ms. McKay makes everyone hard like that," Emily said, looking down at his cock.

"I know I'm hard for her most of the time," Lola added in her husky voice.

"What's going on, Emily?" Andy stammered. "Why did you make me come here?"

"I don't think you've cum yet," Lola said, licking her lips.

"Don't tease him, Lola. He's been through so much already, poor dear," Emily said, playfully spanking Lola's round ass.

Lola wiggled and let out a long purr. She slipped one hand between her legs. Andy gulped, his eyes locked on Lola's fingers as she traced her mound through the black satin.

"I've already decided, as you know, that the proper punishment for your indiscretion was to watch me get off while you couldn't touch yourself," Emily said. "But now I think that you watching me fuck Edward isn't good enough. You need a stiffer punishment."

"He looks pretty stiff right now," Lola giggled.

"Of course, he is, Lola," Emily said, bumping Lola with her hip. "You're fingering yourself right in front of him. That's too cruel."

Lola shrugged, but she didn't stop rubbing her fingers between her legs.

"Anyway," Emily said. "I think an even more appropriate punishment would be for you to watch me with Lola."

"Since you already watched me getting fucked by Cole. How did you like that, Andy? Hot, wasn't it?" Lola teased.

"What do you think about that, Andy?" Emily asked. "Would that be enough punishment if you had to watch me and Lola fuck each other?"

Andy looked from Emily to Lola and back to Emily. Lola stepped close behind Emily and slipped her arms around her middle. Emily turned her head, and they kissed. Lola slid her hand down Emily's flat stomach, over the waistband of her satin panties, down the front, and she cupped Emily's mound. Emily sighed and arched her back.

"Yes," Andy gulped, watching transfixed as Lola gently squeezed Emily's pussy.

"He said yes, Emily," Lola said, purring in Emily's ear.

They kissed. It was a slow kiss with dancing tongues.

"He has no idea what he's in for, Lola," Emily said when their kiss finally broke.

She closed her eyes, reached over her head, and tangled her fingers in Lola's black hair. She pressed her butt against Lola's crotch. Lola had one hand between Emily's legs, rubbing her pussy, and her other hand was on Emily's breast, her fingers squeezing her nipple through the shirt. Their bodies rocked together in a practiced familiar way that

128

hinted at many such couplings in the past. Emily threw back her head, and Lola kissed her neck. Emily untangled her hands from Lola's hair and cupped her other breast, pinching her nipple, and her other hand fell on top of Lola's hand between her legs. Together they rubbed Emily's eager pussy.

Andy groaned and ran his hand up and down his shaft.

"Oh, look, Emily, he's touching himself," Lola whispered.

Emily's eyes fluttered open. She blinked, as if remembering where she was. She looked down at Andy and shook her head.

"No touching," she moaned, and her body bucked as Lola slipped her hand under her waistband and parted her wet folds.

"Ok," Andy stammered, dropping his hands to his side.

"No touching us and no touching yourself," Emily said breathlessly, spreading her legs as Lola's finger slid inside her. "Agreed?"

"Yes," he moaned, watching his wife get fingered by her best friend.

Lola rubbed and fingered Emily's pussy. Emily's body arched and writhed. Andy watched and suffered.

"Oh, Lola," Emily whimpered, her body quivering.

"Are you going to cum, Emily?" Lola whispered, biting Emily's ear. Emily spun around and pulled Lola close. She humped her thigh while she kissed her.

"You're a tease, Lola," she breathed, grinding vigorously on Lola's leg.

"I'll show you teasing, Emily," Lola giggled, and she pushed Emily back.

They stumbled off the runway and collapsed on the chaise next to Andy. Lola was on top, kissing and biting Emily. Emily moaned and rocked her body. Andy gaped as Lola pushed up Emily's top and sucked and bit Emily's nipples. Emily ground her pussy into Lola's knee.

"Fuck, Lola, stop being such a tease," Emily moaned, pushing Lola down.

Lola rained kisses down Emily's body and teased her belly button with her tongue. Then she ran her tongue over the waistband of Emily's satin panties, kissing down the front of the panties. Emily spread her legs wide, lifting her heels in the air, and Lola lowered herself down between her legs and pressed her nose into Emily's mound.

"Ooo," Emily cooed, pulling Lola's hair.

Lola pressed her tongue into the panties. Emily growled and pulled the panties to the side, exposing her pussy. Lola grinned and licked, a long, flat tongue lick, over Emily's slit. Emily bucked.

"She tastes so good," Lola said, eyeing Andy.

Andy trembled.

Lola ran her tongue through Emily's pink folds and slowly circled Emily's swollen bud with the tip of her tongue.

"Watch her closely, Andy," Emily sighed, looking at Andy. "Lola knows

130

what she's doing…" Her words broke when Lola slipped her thumb in her pussy.

Lola licked up and down and slid her thumb in and out of Emily's dripping pussy. Emily bucked. Andy watched. Then Lola slipped her thumb out of Emily's pussy and slid it down to her ass. Emily stopped moving. Lola slowly slid her slick thumb into Emily's ass. Emily groaned and started to shake, shifting her body back and forth. She rode Lola's thumb making it slide in and out of her ass.

"I'm going cum," Emily shrieked, and her body quivered repeatedly as her orgasm raged through her.

Lola pressed her tongue on Emily's clit, and she kept pressing gently until Emily stopped twitching and her breathing settled down.

"That's how it's done, Andy," Lola said. She grinned up at him, her face slick with Emily's juices.

Andy could only moan.

"Get up here," Emily growled, pulling Lola to her.

Lola slid across Emily's body, and they kissed. Lola spread her legs for Emily. Emily grabbed Lola's ass and pulled her close.

"Your turn," Emily snarled, kissing Lola.

"Yes, please," Lola giggled.

They rolled over, Emily on top. They kissed, while Emily ground her body into Lola's.

"Who's the tease now?" Lola groaned, wrapping her legs around Emily's middle.

"I'll show you how teasing is done," Emily said, kissing and nibbling down Lola's body.

"Mmmm," Lola groaned. "No one licks pussy better than your wife, Andy."

Andy gulped.

Emily got up on her knees. "Turn over, Lola," she growled. "I want your ass."

Lola giggled, and flipped on her belly. Emily straddled the back of her legs.

"Do you miss it?" Lola moaned, lifting her butt toward Emily.

"I do," Emily giggled, putting her hands on Lola's hips.

She hooked her fingers in Lola's waistband and pulled the panties over the round of her ass. Then she bent over and licked up Lola's slit and over her ass. Lola moaned. Emily licked. Lola wiggled. Andy shuddered.

"You should have brought Edward," Lola said, pushing her ass back into Emily's face.

"You need dick, Lola?" Emily snarled, and speared Lola's pussy with her tongue. "My tongue's not enough for you?"

Lola thrust back. "I love your tongue, Emily, but I need something deeper," she moaned.

"We've got Andy's cock," Emily hissed. She reached out and closed her fist around Andy's shaft. "It's handy and it's hard."

Lola reached out and closed her fist right above Emily's. There was enough cock left for another fist. Involuntarily, Andy thrust, his cock sliding inside their two fists.

"He's anxious, Lola," Emily laughed.

"And he's bigger than Edward," Lola sighed, rolling her hips back into Emily.

"Thicker, too," Emily said. "Do you want that cock to fill you up, Lola?"

"I'm not saying no, Emily," Lola moaned. "I need something inside me."

Emily laughed, and then she looked at Andy.

"Time to be useful, Andy," she said, getting off Lola. "Move your ass over here and fill up this tight pussy." And she slapped Lola's ass. Lola snarled and lifted up her butt.

"What?" Andy gasped.

"Do I need to tell you twice, Andy?" Emily said. "Get on top of her and fuck her pussy."

"Come on, Andy, my pussy's so wet," Lola moaned. "I need a dick inside me."

Andy didn't need to be told twice. He was up in an instant. He positioned himself behind Lola and put his hands on her hips. The head of his cock pointed at her pink entrance.

"Are you ready to show Lola why I married you, Andy?" Emily giggled, taking his cock in her hand.

"Yes," Andy moaned, as Emily rubbed the head of his cock up and down Lola's wet slit, sliding his head through her folds.

Somehow, Andy got even harder and Lola seemed to sense it. "Stop teasing me, Emily," Lola snarled, looking back over her shoulder, her hunger tangible.

"Are you sure you're ready, Lola? He's so big." Emily grinned. "He'll stretch that tight pussy of yours."

"That's what I need, Emily," Lola moaned, arching her back and wiggling her bum.

The head of Andy's cock throbbed as Emily slid him over Lola's pink entrance.

"You heard her, Andy. She's ready. Fuck her," Emily ordered.

Not needing any more coaxing, Andy slowly slid his throbbing cock inside Lola's wet pussy. She was tight and hot and slick. He moved slow and steady, spreading her open. She hissed, and her legs quivered.

"Oooo," Lola moaned, as Andy sank deeper and deeper inside her.

"Deeper, Andy," Emily ordered, slapping his ass.

Andy thrust to the hilt driving his cock in as deep as he could go. Lola let out a cry, and she dug her nails into Andy's thigh.

"Is he too much for you, Lola?" Emily giggled, moving close to Lola.

"No way," Lola moaned, and the two women kissed, their tongues dancing. "I want more. I want it harder."

"Come on, Andy. Show her what you've got," Emily snarled, and then she pressed her lips against Lola's.

Andy pulled out, his eyes torn between watching his slick cock slide out of Lola's wetness and Emily and Lola kissing. Growling, he thrust his cock back inside Lola. She rocked back to meet his thrust.

"Fuck, you're so tight," Andy gasped.

"My husband likes your pussy, Lola," Emily giggled, as Andy thrust in and out of Lola.

"Oh, that's so good," Lola moaned as Andy rode her.

"Fuck her, Andy," Emily growled.

He fucked Lola till she collapsed in a mass of quivers and moans.

"Oh, I needed that," Lola gasped, grinning.

Emily laughed.

"And you wondered why I married him," Emily said.

"It's all perfectly clear why," Lola whispered.

"Don't think you've seen it all yet, Lola," Emily snorted. "Andy is capable of a lot more. Aren't you, Andy?"

"Absolutely," he said, and he reached down and pulled Emily to him. "I need your pussy. Now."

He pushed her down on top of Lola, ass up.

"What do you think you're doing, Andy?" Emily giggled.

I'm going to fill you like Edward can't," he said, sliding his cock into her.

**

They fucked for what seemed like hours until they were all spent. Then they lay on the chaise, Andy on his back, Emily and Lola sprawled across him, cum shining everywhere.

"Don't forget you're being punished," Emily said, kissing him.

"I won't forget," Andy said, kissing her back.

"Does that mean we're not having any more sex?" Lola asked, her hand closing on Andy's shaft.

He was getting hard again.

"Of course, we're having more. Andy needs to learn his lesson and never forget it," Emily said.

~~~

A word from the author

Hello dear readers,

I'm Misty MacAllister and I'm an erotic writer (this feels very much like an AA meeting). I wanted to take the opportunity to say a little something about myself, the obligatory bio, but that turned out to be harder to do than I thought, so instead I'm going to answer a few of the most common questions I'm asked. Usually I get these questions on social media, where you can go and follow me—please, follow me, Instagram, Facebook, Twitter, and Tumblr—or you can go to MistyMacBookstore.

The number one question is: Do you write from experience?

The answer is no. If I did everything in my stories, when would I have the time to write? And if somehow I had time, I'd be too sore for anything other than a long bubble bath and a glass of wine. The only books I can think of that bear any resemblance to reality are "Pollinate My Flower", because I had an experience with a bumble bee hive when I was little, but those stings weren't nearly as erotic as the stings in the said story, and "An Intimate Encounter of the Fifth Kind", because I sometimes think that my husband is an alien, just without all the extra tentacles. Oh, and "The Bride of Bigfoot". I don't know about you but my hiking experiences have been pretty close to those described in "The Bride of Bigfoot" except for the Bigfoot part, naturally.

The number two question is: Why do you write erotica?

Why not is the easy answer, but the more Freudian answer would be that writing erotica is a manifestation of one of my quirks. I like to peek into houses and hotel windows. I'm not a peeping Tammy, mind you; I always stay on the sidewalk. What I'm really hoping to see is someone, or preferably two someones, doing something naughty (hotel windows seem to me the most likely to produce results). So I guess that's why I write erotica, because not enough people are doing naughty things in their windows and I have to use my imagination. So it's on you, people. Start getting frisky in windows if you want me to stop writing.

The other questions I get are as follows, in no particular order:

Do you work out?
Are you married?
Do you want to meet?
Are you afraid of the dark?
Can you undo knots?
Have you ever been tied up?
Do you want to be tied up?
Etc.

If you want to know the answers, or if you want to check out my other books, you'll have to go to MistyMacBookstore.

Sincerely,
Misty